Whittaker's Theatricals

Cover: The author's design for the landmark production of Brecht's *Galileo,* also directed by him for Jupiter Theatre, Toronto at the ROM Theatre, December 1950. John Drainie and Bernard Raxlen played Galileo and the boy Andrea. Also in the cast were Lorne Greene, Aileen Seaton, David Gardner, Hugh Webster and Leslie Rubie. This first showing in Canada was the second production of the Bertolt Brecht play.

Whittaker's Theatricals

HERBERT WHITTAKER

Foreword by

R. H. Thomson

Toronto, Canada

The writing of this manuscript and the publication of this book were made possible by support from several sources. We would like to acknowledge the generous assistance and ongoing support of **The Canada Council, The Book Publishing Industry Development Program** of the **Department of Communications, The Ontario Arts Council,** and **The Ontario Publishing Centre** of the **Ministry of Culture, Tourism and Recreation**.

Kirk Howard, President; Marian M. Wilson, Publisher

ISBN 0-88924-239-9
1 2 3 4 5 • 8 7 6 5 4

Simon & Pierre Publishing Co. Ltd., a subsidiary of Dundurn Press

Canadian Cataloguing in Publication Data

Whittaker, Herbert, 1910-
Whittaker's Theatricals

Includes bibliographical references
ISBN 0-88924-239-9

1. Actors—Canada—Biography.
2. Theatre—Canada.
3. Theatre—Canada—History—20th century.
I. Title.

PN2307.W45 1993 792'.028'0922 C92-095565-7

General Editor: Marian M. Wilson
Editor: Richard Horenblas
Indexer: Claudia Willetts
Proofreader: Joe Doucet

Design and Production: Andy Tong

Printed and bound in Canada by Gagné Printing Ltd., Louiseville, Quebec, Canada

Order from Simon & Pierre Publishing Co. Ltd., care of

Dundurn Press Limited
2181 Queen Street East
Suite 301
Toronto, Canada
M4E 1E5

Dundurn Distribution
73 Lime Walk
Headington, Oxford
England
0X3 7AD

Dundurn Press Limited
1823 Maryland Avenue
P.O. Box 1000
Niagara Falls, N.Y.
U.S.A. 14302-1000

For
Sir John Gielgud
In Admiration

"Shakespeare is a savage with some imagination, whose plays can please only in London and Canada."
—Voltaire, writing in 1765

Other Books by
HERBERT WHITTAKER

The Stratford Festival 1953-57.
Toronto: Clarke, Irwin & Company, 1958

Canada's National Ballet.
Toronto: McClelland & Stewart Inc., 1967

Preface to *Modern Canadian Drama.*
Toronto: Penguin Books Canada Ltd. 1984

Whittaker's Theatre 1944-1975,
edited by Ronald Bryden.
Toronto: The Whittaker Project, 1985

Winston's: The Life and Times of a Great Restaurant,
co-author with Arnold Edinborough.
Toronto: Stoddart, Publishing Co. Ltd. 1988

Acknowledgments

A lifetime of acknowledgments, most immediately to my editor Richard Horenblas for his insistence on contemporary punctuation and other matters. Indeed, to all my past editors and proof readers I must give the nod—from Adam Marshall and Iain Dow at *The Gazette* to Eldon Stonehouse and Donn Downey at *The Globe and Mail.*

And to other newspapermen—such as Charles Peters, S. Morgan-Powell, Robert Farquharson, Oakley Dalguish, Kaspar Dzeguze, Charles Taylor, R. R. Duffy and Senator Richard Doyle—my gratitude for their tolerance. To members of critics' circles—Thomas Archer, John Fraser, Sydney Johnson, Jack Karr, Philip Hope-Wallace, Brooks Atkinson, Clive Barnes, Mavor Moore, Charles Haines, Robin Breon and Jeniva Berger from the Drama Bench and the Canadian Theatre Critics Association—my appreciation. I would also like to mention *The Gazette* and *The Globe and Mail*, two top employers.

More direct help came from Alex Barris, Susan Benson, Ronald Bryden, Anna Cameron, Arthur Carveth, Stephen Churnin, Edgar Andrew Collard, Hugh Davidson, Robertson Davies, Ed Du Rocher, Glen Frankfurter, Tammy Grimes, Garrick Hagon, Michael Holroyd, Mary Joliffe, Eric McLean, David Mirvish, John Primm, Jonathan Rittenhouse, Gillian Rugheimer, Hugh Walker, Leonard White, Rosamund Young and, of course, that one person I'm sure I left out.

Last but not least, I am grateful to my nephew, Jeffrey Whittaker, and the members of my family who have long put up with my obsession with theatre, starting with my mother, Eleanor Trappitt Whittaker, who put me on to it in the first place. Bless her.

Herb Whittaker

Herbert Whittaker
Toronto 1993

TABLE OF CONTENTS

LIST OF ILLUSTRATIONS

Foreword

by R.H. Thomson

Herbert Whittaker's path and my own have crossed many times. He has entered my life and career at timely moments, and each time he has introduced me to perspectives on the professions we have each circled so arduously. His is a view that I have long appreciated. It encompasses a long span of time in Canadian theatre whose content is now extremely lively.

Sometimes I credit myself with precocious instinct. Even at a pre-school age, I sought the inside track with the eminent critic from The Globe and Mail. It was in the Lion's Club Hall of my home town. The Curtain Club was presenting a three night run of *The Chalk Garden* and my mother was producing. I should mention that life in my home often became overbearingly intimate with these community productions—to this day, I recall much of the first page of dialogue of High Ground, learnt as a six year old lolling on the basement floor during rehearsals. It was perhaps to impress this notable critic from Toronto, Mr. Herbert Whittaker, that I was more than casually involved in the production of *The Chalk Garden.* At an appropriate moment in Act II, when the butler was performing some minor dusting on stage, I tugged at the critic's sleeve, pointing to the prop duster, and breathlessly informed him that "those were my pajamas!" Whether this incident indicated to him the small possible career which sat beside him at that moment, he has never told me.

As I introduced Herbie to my pajamas, so he introduced me to classical Greek theatre. He had the audacity to cast me, at seventeen, as the leader of the chorus of male ancients in *Lysistrata* when I was a student at the University of Toronto. Masked and trembling with age, we descended the aisles of Hart House Theatre chanting "Lysi-STRATA" in our most masculine voices, while on stage our director had instructed our female half to counter us with chants of "Ly-SIS-trata."

Herbie's was the critical voice that I often looked to for understanding and encouragement during my early days in theatre, whether navigating new Canadian work at the Alumnae Theatre—himself directing—or in his critical encouragements of me in print. He sometimes covered university productions for The Globe and Mail, and his proddings put me in mind of the world beyond the university stage, namely the professional stage in Canada. Of course, the moment one considered a professional career, by an all-too-easy corollary came the thoughts of the professional world beyond in New York and London. It seems to be a knot that each artist in this land must wrestle with. By whose standards shall we judge our work, and in whose world must our art appear? Is the "culture" in Toronto (or Regina or Halifax) energetic and broad-based enough to support the ambitions of our lives, or must we leave our roots behind, as so many have done before? For myself, each time that I return to the Canadian "knot," it disturbs the purposes behind my career: Why am I doing it? Why must I do it?

So bumping into the critical, yet friendly, face of H.W. Whittaker in the dress circle of a London theatre was important to me in my massaging of the "knot." Just as useful were the provocations from the walls of his

Toronto apartment, crowded as they are with prints of past theatre. Each time I visit, actors stare at me from his walls. They are sometimes centuries dead, yet their printed presences remind me that mine is an ancient profession, and that my theatrical masters should be not only the producers and directors of the present but also the artists and writers of the past. Their stares and the faded playbills lining the walls demand that I keep the faith. They will me to pass on the body and the holiness of the theatre. Their stares insist that, if I am privileged enough, I must shoulder some of the great characters, bridging their lives to yet another generation. I hope that, in time, I too may "will" from someone's wall, staring from the other side.

I will also pass on the "knot," as those who have gone before me have. We Canadians know that ours will never be a dominating culture. Our riddle is always to what degree we will be dominated. For how long will we gravitate in someone else's sphere? This has always been and continues to be part of the Canadian "knot." Each artist must deal with it in his or her own way. Glenn Gould was said to have thought that as a musician it was his goal to have people listen. If they would only listen to him, they might hear the music he was hearing, on and between and beneath the notes. In a similar way, in this transitory role of an actor; my real purpose is to use whatever powers or artistry I have to bring people to hear the stories of the world—to hear the stories beyond and beneath the plots, the story of our own beginnings. These are the stories of creation.

I crossed my path not long ago with Herbie Whittaker's when I invited him to be on the advisory committee of the International Theatre Festival that I organized in 1992. I was delighted by the gusto with which he took up the challenge, meeting me head on in some of our more contentious decisions. But then again, that was the person who had prodded me so many times before. How right it was to have him with me on this latest stage of turning out to the world, returning to the "knot" once more, and for me to realize once again—but yet more deeply—what a country we have here in our home and native land.

It is now appropriate that a book of this nature appear, given that we may at last be passing over the watershed—the one that allured so many artists into leaving their homes to achieve their art. How often I have considered all the wonderful talents that we have lost. What would our lives have been like if they had all stayed here?

RH Thomson

Introduction

by Herbert Whittaker

When I was first appointed drama critic for *The Globe and Mail*, I wanted to demonstrate that Canadian talent was equal to any in the outside world. I wrote articles about Canadian successes abroad and balanced these with dramatic incidents in our own theatre. On occasion, Canadians contributed to the glamour and excitement of international theatrical life. Sometimes, the most glamourous and exciting figures of that world came here and took part in our theatrical life.

Over the years, I collected stories of such involvements. Some I used in my column "Showbusiness," until I perceived that it could better serve a growing theatre if I just recorded the activities of our own artists at home. But I always regretted cutting off that flow of what my friends call, quite accurately, name-dropping. Now, I think the time has come to drop a few names.

I began on the invitation of the Arts and Letters Club, where I read a piece recalling my involvement with names such as Charles Laughton and Bertolt Brecht. The audience at that literary luncheon in May 1991 was complimentary, and I was persuaded that others might also enjoy knowing about the Canadian angle to international theatre.

Since then I have been going through old notes and files, my own and others,' researching, writing and typing the manuscript. By the way, my typing is appalling, the result of a newspaper life sheltered by protective editors, typographers and proofreaders. I'm told I wouldn't get away with it today.

And now you have in your hands Whittaker's Theatricals, vignettes of Canadian theatre and its personalities. I send it off with my thanks to all the members of the Canadian and international theatre communities, and especially the stars of this book, for the wonderful memories they have given me.

The Lives of Galileo

The Life of Galileo, here and there. This is in the nature of an exploration of Toronto's theatrical past, but it also involves two book reviews and two play reviews. One of the books is an actor's biography by an actor, the other the chronicle of a play's production in London. All concern Bertolt Brecht's *The Life of Galileo*, this being the link.

Brecht is the abiding genius of this investigation, although he appears only as a secondary figure in the biography. The most revolutionary and still the most controversial dramatist of our century, he had escaped from the Nazis to Denmark in 1938 when he started his study of Galileo with one Ferdinand Reyher, an American. Brecht is unique among playwrights in his welcoming of collaborators. He was to welcome a more famous one when his escape took him to Hollywood with other noted German refugees.

I start my story a few summers ago with one of those pleasures known only to lovers of low-priced books. At a Bloor Street shop east of Avenue Road, I came across a theatre book I had never heard of, though it was published in 1981. Written by Jim Hiley, it is titled *Theatre at Work*, and it is a remarkably well documented account of a stage production in London: the National Theatre's 1980 production of Brecht's *Galileo*.

Rarely has such a detailed study of the components and procedures of any production been set down. Hiley interviewed carpenters, welders, publicists as well as actors in an investigation of how the full resources of the new National Theatre's Olivier Theatre were being used to serve a vast and strange new play. He details the problems between various craft unions and stage management, the vacillations of the designer, Jocelyn Herbert, who faced new problems every day, and the anguish of young actors under a demanding, almost devilish director, John Dexter. (You may remember that Dexter was blocked in 1980 from becoming artistic director of our Stratford Festival by our Immigration Department.)

Sir Peter Hall was eager to stage Brecht's biggest play in the National's largest theatre, which features a very wide, very open stage. As a Marxist, Brecht had wanted to establish an epic People's Theatre. Hall, head of the National Theatre, called in a new British playwright, Howard Brenton, to retranslate *The Life of Galileo.* Himself a Marxist, Brenton could be counted on to do Brecht justice.

Everything that could go wrong seems to have gone wrong with this production, all of it exaggerated by the size of the stage and the pressure of other demands on a repertory theatre system such as the National's.

To cap it all, Sir Peter chose a secondary character actor to undertake the massive central role of Galileo. His choice made Michael Gambon into a star overnight, as The New Yorker chronicled in a profile of the actor. By the time I saw the National's *Galileo* in August 1980, most of its technical problems had been ironed out and I was able—from my seat high above the stage—to admire the munificence of the production. I could also appreciate that most admirable actor, Michael Gambon, as Brecht's Galileo, estranged from the Holy Roman Church by a curiosity that was itself divine. But my major impression remains of a huge panorama of Italian history spread over a wide revolving and sliding platform. The National was using its full stage facilities for the first time and was employing some other splendid actors including Basil Hensen, Mark Digham and Simon Callow.

While enjoying that production, I was distracted by a sharp memory. I was cast back nearly four decades to the tiny walled-in stage of the basement lecture hall in Toronto's Royal Ontario Museum. It was there I had staged this same epic play for the Jupiter Theatre, making its debut in 1951. How had we dared? How had we succeeded? At least we had managed to make John Drainie's Galileo the centre of our universe, tiny though it was. Being a critic, I have learned that comparisons are indeed "odorous," as Dogberry puts it. But I may have distracted myself from the National Theatre's full achievement.

Back to that Bloor Street bookstore in the summertime. Still in search of inexpensive but interesting books I come across a paperback called *Charles Laughton: A Difficult Actor*. The author's name is familiar to me: Simon Callow. I quickly flip to see if there is any reference made in the index to Laughton and the Jupiter Theatre's production of *Galileo*. None. I buy the paperback anyway, knowing there has been one important connection.

This is another book I can recommend highly, for it takes you deep into an actor's mind. Rarely, indeed, has any actor been so articulate about another one. Simon Callow understands Laughton better than any non-actor could, being himself a character actor who achieved stardom and also being homosexual, as Laughton was. He makes no sensational point of that fact as a journalist might, but uses it to delve into the actor's mystique: the flawed artist as unique instrument.

His material is exciting, covering Laughton's meteoric rise as an actor in London, then on from West End and film stardom to Hollywood fame. Films such as *On The Spot*, *The Private Lives of Henry VIII*, The *Hunchback* of *Notre Dame*, *The Barretts of Wimpole Street*, *Les Miserables*, *Mutiny on the Bounty*, and *Rembrandt* all feature remarkable portrayals by Laughton. But the stage still haunted him, and he showed new talent as a platform performer, reading to troops first. As his film career thinned out, Laughton created the First Drama Quartet with Charles Boyer, Agnes Moorhead and Sir Cedric Hardwicke, playing the "Don Juan in Hell" segment from Shaw's *Man and Superman.*

It was this successful venture that brought Laughton to Toronto's Massey Hall in 1951. But before we make that connection, let me point out that Callow's biography records a major event and influence on Laughton in Hollywood: his meeting with Bertolt Brecht. Callow quotes another biographer who claims Laughton "fell in love with Brecht." But their passion lay in collaboration, producing not merely a translation (for which Laughton is credited) but a revision—an elevation of Brecht's earlier *Galileo* script.

This final version of *The Life of Galileo* was strengthened by the added new role of the scientist, imposed by the dropping of the atom bomb on Hiroshima. Brecht was galvanized by Hiroshima, which split the scientist from the rest of the community. Laughton, less political, grasped the theatrical values of this as they wrote, rewrote and edited.

Three years later, with Laughton making minor films

to subsidize *Galileo*, the new script was ready for production. Orson Welles was interested in directing, Billy Rose in producing. But neither one survived the complicated input of Laughton and Brecht. First staged in a small Hollywood theatre with young actors, the play was taken by T. Edward Hambleton to a small Broadway theatre where it lasted four weeks. Meanwhile Brecht, having stonewalled his way out of an investigation by the House Un-American Activities Committee, had fled the United States.

Hambleton claimed that "Laughton's performance in the theatre paled by comparison with his reading of the whole play." And that is just what Charles Laughton did in 1951 for the Jupiter Theatre in Toronto. Our production came so soon after the original one that we worked from the same typed script (later copyrighted in 1952). How did Laughton happen to come here? We knew he was touring in *Don Juan in Hell,* but how did he arrive at Lorne Greene's Academy of Radio Arts during the rehearsal period for *Galileo*?

For that matter, how did Jupiter Theatre, composed of radio-oriented performers led by Lorne Greene and John Drainie, come to choose Brecht's play to begin their first season? Their selection committee, seeking plays that expressed a different point of view, consisted of Drainie, playwright Len Peterson, and businessman Glen Frankfurter. Today, Frankfurter gives the credit for the discovery of *Galileo* to Drainie, who perhaps had read about it in Theatre Arts, the stage's Bible of the day.

"We were looking for plays that expressed our social point of view," Glen says. They had no knowledge of Brecht's communist convictions, but Glen says "it wouldn't have made any difference if we had." The producing group was not afraid of being considered leftist.

For some reason, Toronto looked to Montreal as being more theatrically advanced; and so Jupiter Theatre invited three Montreal directors to stage its plays in that first season. I was already in Toronto, having just come to *The Globe and Mail* from Montreal, so I was offered *Galileo.* I didn't know what I'd gotten myself into—the size of this epic play nor the involvement of the theatre's board of directors (all very active artistically rather than on the business side). Much less was I aware of the Brechtian concept of *Verfremdungseffekt*, which means "making strange" or seeing in a new way. As Brecht put it, "The actor appears in a double role—as Laughton and as Galileo."

We learned to see things from the Brechtian angle as we rehearsed. Drainie as Galileo had what Brecht wanted and what Laughton gave. Since Drainie was lame, I made it easier for him, and kept him still in the centre of my epic world on the tiny basement stage. (I boast that I was trained on small stages and directed Chekhov's *The Seagull* and Shaw's *Heartbreak House* on a platform only half the size of the Museum's stage.)

Having experience in such matters, I designed a cunning setting that gave me full use of that small space: a flat arched cut-out combining suggestions of St. Peter's Rome and the modern observatory. I also pushed an apron out into the house for the crowd scene, flanked by Italian city-state banners to suggest location. I also had the finest of Toronto actors to choose from. Best of all, I had John Drainie.

What we lacked in experience in the exotic world of Brecht, we absorbed on one historic afternoon in late 1951 when the Jupiter Theatre's board invited Charles

Laughton to read his translation of Bertolt Brecht's *The Life of Galileo*.

Laughton's own mannered acting was familiar, made more so by the hundreds of people who thought they could imitate him. His "Mister Christian" was a by-word. The fact that you could see him "acting" was what appealed to Brecht, for he wanted the audience to see the actor and the character simultaneously, the actor both performing and making a comment. All of my Jupiter actors who could get the afternoon off were treated to a hypnotizing and comprehensive communication of Brecht's *Galileo* by the best man in the world to do it. By the man who could make a mere reading better than a whole Broadway production.

Those who were there that day remember different things. I recall the economy of his female impersonation: a finger to the chin and a drop of a curtsy was all he did to tell you it was a woman speaking. Everybody remembers his impersonation of the Old Cardinal, for which two of my cast had to support him, convincing us that old cardinals don't fade away but struggle valiantly to be heard. The board had supplied a bottle of scotch and, through the afternoon, Laughton and Drainie retired to a small office to carry out further investigations. Laughton was highly relaxed when Glen Frankfurter drove him back to his hotel with barely time to get to Massey Hall to make up for the performance by his First Drama Quartet.

I went to his hotel after the Massey Hall performance, as arranged, to question Laughton on certain lines of the Brecht script I found beyond me. With a great air of conspiracy, he picked out the passages that baffled me and said the author had included them for his own political reasons; but if I ever repeated that he'd said so, Laughton would deny it. He taught us our *Galileo* very well.

The Laughton version had come under attack. In fact, Orson Welles said in a first-night telegram that the actor was a fraud to claim credit for the translation. Laughton had rejected Eric Bentley's version to make his own translation, painfully, paragraph by paragraph, with Brecht by his side alternating word choices. When I was visiting Berlin in 1957, I was taken to the Eastern sector to visit the Berliner Ensemble theatre. Elisabeth Hauptmann, then running the company with Brecht's widow, said that, when the official English translations came out, they would not be done by Eric Bentley. Hers had been the rough translation that Laughton started work on in Hollywood.

Brecht, poet as well as dramatist, wrote about his collaboration in a poem dedicated to Laughton, written during the war:

"Still your people and mine were tearing each
other to pieces when we
Pored over those tattered exercise books looking
Up words in dictionaries and time after time
Crossed out our texts and then
Under the crossings-out excavated
The original turns of phrase. Bit by bit—
While the housefronts crashed down in our capitals—
The facades of language gave way. Between us
We began following what characters and
actions dictated:
Now text.
Again and again I turned actor, demonstrating
A character's gestures and tone of voice, and you
Turned writer. Yet neither I nor you
Strayed outside his professions."

What we Torontonians witnessed in that little classroom on Jarvis Street was one half of a collaboration, laying it all before us, and we were fortunate that it was the more splendidly communicative of the two. I was sorry that Simon Callow's book didn't include this tiny jot of Canadian theatre history in Laughton's biography, but we were not entirely overlooked in the realm of Brecht.

When David Gardner and I passed through the Berlin Wall in 1957 to visit Brecht's theatre in East Berlin, we were greeted warmly— as the Canadian director and David as the interpreter of the role of Lodovic, fiancé of Galileo's daughter (a role Laughton had persuaded Brecht to turn into an aristocrat). We were welcomed backstage and were served coffee in between seeing the Berliner Ensemble's versions of *Galileo* and the famous *Mother Courage.* The latter production starred Helene Weigel (Madame Brecht), head of the company since Brecht 's death the year before.

In East Berlin, I could make comparisons again. A tall copper cyclorama shaped the stage, with apertures opening to suggest the various locations. Like the later version by England's National Theatre, this one had enormous resources (contributed by the Communist state) at its disposal. Yet I could still recall Jupiter Theatre's 1951 production of *The Life of Galileo* with pride, modest though it was. It had the blessings of Brecht's gifted collaborator, Charles Laughton, and a great Galileo in John Drainie.

Our *Galileo* opened on December 14, 1951, in the middle of Christmas shopping and the worst blizzard in memory. Opened? It exploded. Three dozen of Toronto's best—including Lorne Greene, Eric House, Margot Christie, George Robertson, Aileen Seaton, Hugh Webster, Colin Eaton, David Gardner, Les Rubie and

Donald Glen—erupted onto that small basement stage to evoke the High Renaissance, with Drainie the still centre of a new universe. I put a spotlight on him for his famous recantation, which Brecht had placed off stage. That scene even pleased fellow-critic Nathan Cohen, who approved Jupiter Theatre's choice though not my production.

Yet that Jupiter Theatre production of *Galileo,* I believe, linked Canada to world theatre. Happily, there have been many more such links, more than many Canadians remember. This book will tell you about a few of them.

Sarah Bernhardt

Born in 1844. Trained at the Paris Conservatoire, she made her debut at the Comédie-Française in 1862; transferred to Théâtre Odéon 1863; Coppée's *Le Passant* in 1869, Hugo's *Ruy Blas* in 1872, her first major successes. Returned to Comédie-Française in 1874. Scored heavily as Racine's Phèdre. Toured to London in 1879, to North America in 1880, later to Europe, Russia, Australia. Scored international successes in *La Dame aux camélias*, *Hamlet* and *L'Aiglon*. Died while filming in France in 1923 at age seventy-nine.

Divinity in Montreal

I believe the most flattering way to celebrate a visit by a great player is to write a play about it—granting that the occasion provides sufficiently dramatic material. With Sarah Bernhardt, everything in her life was sufficiently dramatic. She made sure of that in her long career as the world's best-known and most-admired actress. Sure enough, her visit to Montreal in 1880 lived up to her reputation fully.

It consequently inspired a little play before the flurry of Sarah dramatizations that have come along since 1939, when a group of ambitious young Montrealers known as The 16-30 Club produced it. Now this may not have been actually first. About that time, there was a film—roughly based on a play that was based on Bernhardt's career—with Garbo as "The Divine Lady" of its title. But ours was not based on anything so flagrantly fictional.

We called ours *Divinity in Montreal.* Or rather I called it that to conceal what it was about from the other competitors in the Dominion Drama Festival. I was very much involved. In fact, two years before, I had picked up a copy of *Memories of My Life* (Sarah's autobiography, published in 1907) during my first visit to New York. When I came to the chapter headed "I Visit Montreal," I was hooked. "We must have a play for the Festival; and Marjorie Raven (our best actress) must play Sarah," I told colleagues. I was very susceptible to actresses, especially good ones, then as now.

That chapter is, of course, the basis of this memoir of mine. I wish I could recall for you that I once saw the Divine Sarah, but Death snatched her from me. I envied Louis Mulligan (a stalwart with the Montreal Repertory Theatre) for his memory of her last appearance in Montreal, outside the stage door of the now vanished His Majesty's Theatre. "Flaming red hair . . . leopard skin coat, a sedan chair to carry her to her waiting cab, and a wave to her fans. . . ." Never mind, I can do better than that. I can go back to Sarah's own memories of Montreal on that earlier visit and to all of the excitements that made her life so thrilling wherever she went.

For one thing, the Bishop of Montreal had forbidden his parishioners to attend the immoral plays this notorious French actress brought with her. But far from a frosty welcome, she was greeted at the railway station by a band playing "La Marseillaise" and the sound of a thousand throats giving vent to "Hurrah! Long live France!" Music indeed for a woman as patriotic as Sarah proved herself to be throughout her lifetime. Hundreds of flaming torches illuminated the path to the icy platform where waited a tall young French-Canadian poet, unknown to her but already known a little in Paris.

Louis Frechette—for it was indeed he—unfurled a long scroll which began "Salut Sarah! salut charmante Doña Sol" and went on for eight stanzas in a similar vein. In a temperature twenty-two degrees F. below freezing, this was insupportable. So Sarah, naturally, fainted.

Frechette rescued her from the adoring mob of students, leaving a man of enormous size to save her sister Jeanne, when Sarah recovered enough to cry out, "Help! My sister is being killed!" Sarah promptly fainted again in Frechette's arms and didn't come to until she was safe in her suite in the grand Windsor Hotel. That was where we began our little play, which we had invited a friend, Janet Alexandra McPhee, to set down for us. Inside the hotel, waiting journalists learned what had happened outside, and there Sarah met Jeanne's rescuer, who proved every bit as dramatic as Sarah could have wished. "A Hercules, very tall with wide shoulders, small head, a hard look but hair thick and curly, tanned complexion." He was "fine-looking but uneasy" when he brought her a bouquet of violets and begged her to think well of him, no matter what she heard later. Whereupon Sarah's manager, Jarrett, arrived to inform her that her visitor was a murderer sought by the police.

Sarah, who penned these memoirs some twenty-six years later, was able to report most regretfully that Jeanne's saviour had later met his death by hanging. "The anger of the Bishop of Montreal was necessary to enable me to regain my good humour," she added, giving us an indication of the mercurial personality we were attempting to recapture in our play.

The Bishop's principal target in the Bernhardt repertoire was Eugene Scribe's high romance, *Adrienne Lecouvreur*, denounced from the pulpit as "immoral," "adulterous" and, even worse, containing the character of an abbé, which constituted a direct insult to the clergy. You can imagine how Sarah reacted to that particular denunciation. Gleefully!

Gleefully, too, she recalls that not only *Adrienne Lecouvreur* but also *Froufrou*, *La Dame aux camélias* and *Hernani* were colossal successes with the Montreal public, bringing in fabulous receipts to which Sarah was always partial. Sarah's good temper was indeed restored and she went off (presumably on Sunday) to Ottawa. So did Frechette, the poet who joined her entourage along with Jeanne, Jarrett and Edouard Angelo, the handsome leading man whose only fault was his inability to act. "The only thing he lacked," as she herself put it, "was talent." This excursion had its excitement too, what with four carriages crossing the frozen St. Lawrence River. But it also had its depressing aspect, as it turned out.

Was it Caughnawauga which provided a visit to "the chief, father and mayor of the Iroquois tribes"? It was a depressing introduction, because this son of the mighty Big White Eagle was clothed in rags and reduced to selling liquor, thread, needles, flax, pork fat and chocolate, according to the observant Sarah. She met his plain daughter, too. "I was in a hurry to leave the store–the home of these two victims of civilization. I returned to Montreal somewhat sad and tired." Sarah was no shallow queen of the stage. Her observations are often deep and compassionate, and it is not hard to understand her notable record during the war when she ran her own hospital.

She was to be cheered again, and this time by the devotion of the Montreal students. They mastered the art of adulation when they tied their sonnets and their great compliments with ribbons around the necks of doves that flew down to the stage after each performance. And, using strings that guided baskets of flowers in the same direction, they formed choirs to sing out her praises. "Most of them," Sarah remembered, "were gifted with magnificent voices."

The great moment for her came on opening night when hundreds of young male voices roared out "La Marseillaise" in tribute to their beloved, charming and famous visitor from France.

Perhaps their demonstration was also for the benefit of the Governor General. The Marquis of Lorne stood at attention through the tribute of their visitor's national anthem, and so did the rest of the house. "I do not believe I ever heard 'La Marseillaise' sung with keener emotion and unanimity," Sarah wrote all those years later. But she was moved to respect by Lorne's punctilious behavior. "As soon as it was over . . . upon a sharp gesture from him, the orchestra struck up 'God Save the Queen.' I never saw a prouder and more dignified gesture than that of the Governor," she noted. "He was quite willing to allow these sons of submissive Frenchmen [which is the way Sarah saw them] to feel a regret, perhaps even a flickering hope . . . but he smothered the last echo beneath the English national anthem. Being English, he was incontestably right to do so." Besides, she was well aware that his wife, the Marchioness of Lorne, was a daughter of Queen Victoria herself. So Lorne was insisting that proper respect be paid to his venerable mother-in-law.

Sarah's exit from Montreal was satisfying and typical. She sent a donation to the Bishop, thanking him for the welcome she had been given by his parishioners. On that note she left, knowing that she would always find an audience in Montreal, not only one that loved her but also one that understood the plays she was acting in America.

It was a pity that The 16-30 Club couldn't crowd such high dramatic events onto its tiny church-hall stage at the Church of the Messiah. But what we took to festival audiences proved acceptable enough. The adjudicator, British actor George Skillan, named Marjorie Raven as best actress in the Western Quebec region. He also sent *Divinity in Montreal* on to compete in Ottawa. Our small company—Tom MacBride, Doug Peterson, Betty Taylor and Rae Guess, with me as both designer and director, and Jan Raven as stage manager—was thrilled.

We didn't have such good luck in Ottawa. It turned out that the adjudicator of the finals, critic S. R. (Robin) Littlewood, had met Sarah when he was a young man sheep-farming in Australia as she came touring. He could not accept our portrayal of Sarah, drawn from her own self-portrait, because he remembered her as very practical, interested in sheep-farming. He recognized the worth of our effort, though, and gave Janet's play the Sir Barry Jackson Challenge Trophy for the Best Canadian Play of 1939. But he couldn't endorse our version of the woman he had met so long ago and so far away. He gave the Best Actress award instead to Betty Taylor, who had played Sarah's sister Jeanne.

I can't help thinking that Sarah would have been much amused to know the lasting impression she made on that young Australian sheep-farmer. That would have put her in a very good humour. But her first visit to Montreal gave her a great deal of dramatic satisfaction. That rousing welcome, the murderer, the ecstatic students, the proud Governor General, the fallen Chief, the furious Bishop—not to mention risking her life on the ice floes of the St. Lawrence River—were enough to keep her from being bored. And think of it: that Montreal visit in 1880 lasted only four days!

The Catholic Church had the last word, although it had to wait for it. Many years later, when Sarah was making a farewell tour, another archbishop delivered a sermon denouncing another Bernhardt vehicle, *La Sorcière*, which presented her as a victim of The Inquisition. Not only did he deliver his denunciation, he also had it printed. By the time the company got to Quebec, the antagonism led to pelting the actors with eggs and hurling sticks and stones. In Ottawa, the Governor General apologized to Madame Sarah for such behaviour. Whatever her response to him was, she said in an interview what she really thought: "Canadians, so advanced from so many points of view, are still Iroquois Indians as far as art is concerned."

Edmund Kean

Tragedian, born in 1787 in London. No schooling to speak of. Began his professional career as Cupid at Drury Lane in 1793. Played a demon in *Macbeth* with Sarah Siddons and John Philip Kemble for one night only. Ran away to join Richardson's Circus. Toured theatres in England and Ireland. Played Shylock at Drury Lane in 1814 to great success. Roles included Richard III, Othello, Hamlet, Romeo, King Lear. Visited America in 1820. Second visit in 1826 included Montreal and Quebec. Physical decay set in. Died in 1833 at the age of forty-six.

The Final Impersonation

How does an actor's reputation survive him? Through the impressions of discerning and trustworthy viewers far more than box office returns. And so, Edmund Kean is still rated "England's greatest tragic actor," because of high opinion from contemporary people such as the critic, William Hazlitt. Lord Byron fainted when Kean played Shylock. Samuel Taylor Coleridge declared that seeing Kean act was "like reading Shakespeare by flashes of lightning." "The sensual life of verse springs warm from the lips of Kean," wrote Keats in a criticism printed in *The Champion*. "And one learned in Shakespearean hieroglyphics," adds Oscar Wilde, quoting Keats in *A Critic in Pall Mall*. "Learned in the spiritual portion of those lines to which Keats adds a sensual grandeur. His tongue must seem to have robbed the Hybia bees and left them honeyless."

The acclaim Kean won on his first tour of America in 1820 backed up such opinions. The trouble was that this triumphant progress did not include Canada. *The Gazette*, Montreal's leading English-language paper (then as now), complained about this in an editorial signed Philo Euripides, inviting the tragedian to remedy this next time round. But next time round it was a different Kean, one already showing the signs of much drink. If that wasn't bad enough, he was also pursued by scandals at home (where he seduced an alderman's wife) and showed some

John Wilkes Booth,
possibly 1869

Sarah Bernhardt in 1880
travelling costume

Marjorie Raven in *Divinity in Montreal*, DDF, 1939
illustration by the author

Edmund Kean Reciting Before the Hurons,
oil painting by Joseph Légaré, 1826 (detail)
courtesy Musée des Beaux-Arts de Montréal

Kean's calling card as
Alanienouidet
courtesy National Archives of Canada

Robert Lepage, director of
Marianne Ackerman's 1992 play
photo Les Paparazzi,
courtesy Canadian Opera Company

fraying of the histrionic nerves, not unknown among actors of temperament.

Montreal was to get a full sampling of this in a memorable visit indeed. When one learns from a biography of Marlon Brando that his troubled career found its source in drunken parents, the thought of Kean's background can surely exonerate him for any of his later extravagances. His mother, a Miss Carey, did not declare his father. Edmund Kean, from whom he took his name eventually, may have merely been the man who ran for the midwife. Miss Carey, whose ancestry included the composer of "Sally in Our Alley" and even perhaps "God Save the King" (which didn't stop him from committing suicide), proved an indifferent parent. Her substitute was a kindly Miss Tidswell, who was associated with the premier Catholic peer, the Duke of Norfolk. She loved the little redheaded boy with the piercing black eyes, especially when he recited from Shakespeare, which he did often (this being the age of the Infant Roscius). A Mrs. Clarke left a delightful account of engaging the six year old child to recite for her guests: what a good sense of theatre he displayed, giving an electrifying performance of Richard III.

As a child, he "went on" as a cauldron demon with the great Sarah Siddons and her noble brother, Charles Kemble, in *Macbeth*; but the child's demonic antics did not please. He was let go after one night. Later on, he played in Belfast, married an Irish actress, begat a son, and almost starved to death in the provinces before he finally made Drury Lane at the age of twenty-seven.

In reaching this point, he had suffered many indignities: a disgraceful childhood, running away from starvation to join a circus, breaking both legs, and being involved in countless salary disputes. On that icy day, January 26, 1814, the theatre was only half full. His applause on entrance as a black-wigged Jew was polite until he spat out Shylock's line, "If I can catch him once upon the hip." Then it suddenly changed and theatrical history exploded. Happily, William Hazlitt was in attendance to record that "first gleam of genius breaking athwart the gloom o' the stage." Kean's first entrance, leaning on a cane, was said by Douglas Jerrold to be "like a chapter of Genesis." Then on February 12, 1814, more history was made when he played Richard III, his favourite part. "One of the finest pieces of acting we have ever beheld, or perhaps that the stage has ever known," wrote the anonymous critic of *The Morning Post*. Next came his Hamlet, which won the approval of the eighty year old widow of another great actor, David Garrick. "Mr. Kean," she pronounced, "is like Mr. Garrick himself," and sent him Garrick's stage jewels.

With these credentials, Kean won a vast audience even before he appeared in New York in 1820, where there were riots in the rush for tickets. His subsequent tour brought the same kind of ecstatic response and the same vast crowds. That Montreal, which prided itself then as a major theatre town, was not included in this first visit by the greatest tragedian of his age prompted *The Gazette's* editorial invitation. Next time round, in 1825, *The Gazette* got far more than it ever expected.

The word from New York five years later was warning enough. Kean's physical condition had been sharply reduced; drink and possibly drugs brought incipient madness. At one performance, he could not control an insane laugh, and the curtain was rung down. Yet Montreal still got some measure of the tragedian's former greatness. He opened with his famous Richard III on July 31, 1826, and followed that with Shylock, the role that had made him famous, to electrify the audience packing the Theatre Royal. (This was a new building at Bonsecours Market in 1825, although it was the town's sixth theatre.) He followed this with Othello and Lear. Let it be understood that Kean was supported in all these performances by leading local actors, headed by the Theatre Royal's first manager, Frederick Brown.

Also, the custom of afterpieces was maintained, in which Kean participated. We have the report of one citizen, T.S. Brown, which throws a comic light on the regrettable history, for other viewers had reported on Kean's physical decline. The afterpiece was Robert Elliston's successful burlesque called *Bonaparte*, addressed to that fallen titan but incorporating the titles of popular plays of the day. A curious topicality, it warns the Emperor that "There's the Devil to pay/When he meets up with the English fleet, sir," and then winds up "Humanity's spark will not cool, sir/And the Exile that flies from his rage/Will meet a kind friend in John Bull, sir." All of which was just the stuff to delight a public so soon after Waterloo.

Somehow, the recitation of this lyric by a character called Daggerwood involves the performer standing on his head on a chair. Kean, however, was extremely drunk and failed to make the head-stand. "Another tumble, Mr. Kean," the gallery encouraged him. But Kean thought their cry was "Another tumbler, Mr. Kean." Furious at this ridicule, he left the stage and the theatre. The gallery, insulted, started to smash up the Theatre Royal. So manager Brown ran, presumably, to the Masonic Hall Hotel and found Kean in bed. The actor was forcibly dressed and brought back to the theatre, where he made a graceful apology. But he wound it up saying: "As for the man who told me to take another tumbler, I despise him!" This was given in Kean's deepest and most tragic tones, fairly bringing down the house.

As one of the men at the public banquet which was tendered Kean on this visit, T.S. Brown also leaves an account of the peculiar confession the actor made there. "When I left England," Kean said in responding to the toast, "reason told me I had lost a portion of my respectability as a man, and my chief resources depended on my exertions as an actor. I assumed, therefore, a callous indifference, played for a time the character of a misanthrope, knit my brows, and pretended contempt for the world. But it was merely acting. . . . Deeply I felt the loss of that society I had for years been associated with, and every act of kindness penetrated the brazen armour I had borrowed for the occasion. The searching eye could even discern smiles without mirth and pastime without pleasure." Kean won the sympathy of the Montrealers, and was much feted before he moved on by tugboat to Quebec.

The tugboat, *Hercules*, was delayed and, although announced for Thursday, didn't deliver him until Monday. The public bellman announced the fact, and the theatre was crowded, with the Governor-in-Chief and Lady Dalhousie in the vice-regal box. That engagement at the Royal Circus went well until the final night, when Kean, finding his supporting cast "mediocre," refused to play

Hamlet. Scenes from Otway's *Venice Preserved* were his substitute, which led to another audience riot causing "considerable material damage." The Quebec visit was also marked by an occurrence that was to provide an obsession which lasted the rest of Kean's short life.

Four chiefs of the Wyandot tribe of Hurons attended a performance and expressed a desire to meet him to show him how greatly impressed they were. So Kean entertained them, even reciting and singing for them. In admiration of these "noble savages," he swore that he would like to join their life, leaving the ways of the white man behind. They made him a chief, investing him with magnificent regalia and bestowing on him the tribal name of Alanienouidet (which has been translated as "drifting snow driven by a strong wind"). Kean now decided to renounce the civilization he had known and to become a chief in life. Later, he confessed a madness overcame him. He vanished with his new brothers to the camp at Lorette. That was in late October. A few days later, his friends from the theatre tracked him down and brought him back to Quebec before packing him off to New York.

However, the charade was not over. A Dr. John Francis was summoned to Kean's hotel room in New York. There, he encountered a warrior chief: "His well-shaped head was decked in eagle plumes from behind which masses of black locks flowed. Thick gold rings hung from his nose and ears, his face was streaked with red and yellow paint, a collar of bear skins clasped his neck. Buffalo hides clad his form, his leggings garnished with porcupine quills, his moccasins decorated with beads, his bare arms adorned with shining bracelets. A tomahawk was suspended from his waist, whilst in his hands he held a bow and arrow."

The astonished doctor added that "his eye was meteoric and fearful like the furnace of the Cyclops."

The doctor admitted he was much relieved when this apparition spoke. The voice was unmistakably that of Kean. Dr. Francis declared that "Kean was as rejoiced as a schoolboy at . . . the effect of his costume. He valued the honour the Indians had conferred on him above the highest triumph he had achieved at Drury Lane. [In fact,] he was yet undecided whether he would wholly cast his lot with them or return to London."

The tragedian's final weeks in New York demonstrated physical and mental decline in advanced stages, accompanied by violent spasmodic attacks. That he was suffering deeply, both mentally and physically, "was but too apparent. His powers had declined and, by some of his acquaintances, it was considered he had not long to live." A periodical, *The Albion*, printed that "nothing but a salutary and persevering reform of his social habits could prolong his existence. Possibly, the abstinence of a sea voyage, the counsel of his friends, and the suggestions of his own good sense may work a beneficial change in some of his injurious indulgences." Kean's life was feared for as he sailed for England on December 5 after one last performance as Richard III.

Kean had become obsessed with being a chieftain and a prince of the Huron tribe. He had himself painted in full regalia and made prints of this in Philadelphia, enscribed to the directors of the Theatre Royal, Drury Lane. Another friend from London came upon him at his hotel, similarly bedizened. He observed Kean wearing "a large fur cap decked with many gorgeous feathers on his head, a scalping knife in his belt, and a tomahawk in his hand, whilst an artist painted his portrait as Alanienouidet."

Canada had caught the great actor on the downward turn and had contributed to his decline into a world of make-believe and disrepute. The books on 19th century theatre record his final performance on March 25, 1833, playing Othello at Covent Garden; with his son Charles as Iago. "Kean stood motionless and fixed, his chin resting on his breast, his eyes riveted on the ground. A death-like silence, begotten of fear, fell upon the house . . . he would have fain continued his part, saying: 'Villain, be sure . . . you . . . prove. . . .' Then tottering over to his son, he cried out in a faltering voice, 'Oh God, I am dying. Speak to them, Charles.' For a while, he lay insensible in his dressing room, then was removed to his house in Richmond, where the faithful Miss Tidswell nursed him. In aberration, he relived his early vagabond life, and his triumphs at Drury Lane too. . . . He died speechless!"

The Dean of Westminster Abbey refused Kean the honour of burial beside Garrick, as he had requested. He lies instead in the parish church at Richmond, with church furniture piled across his grave. His tombstone bears the inscription "The Sun's Bright Child"—Byron's tribute. On the wall opposite is a tablet erected by Charles, his respectful and successful son. And not far away lies Richard Burbage, creator of his favourite role.

I remembered that Sarah Bernhardt's visit to Montreal was worthy of a little play. In 1992, Kean's Quebec adventure gave rise to a big one, written, appropriately enough, by a former *Gazette* critic, Marianne Ackerman, with Robert Lepage, the brilliant young director. Called *Alanienouidet* and set in a longhouse, it centres on Kean's Huron connection and the contrast between cultures.

Liam Lacey, one of my successors at *The Globe and Mail*, reviewed *Alanienouidet* at the National Arts Centre in Ottawa. He found it "a dreamy, centrifugal play that radiates from the centre of Kean's disintegrating imagination to form a complex metaphor of colliding cultures." As Kean, he found Randy Hughson to be "a slush-mouthed, randy, drunken, rock star" playing the "brilliant, intensely egocentric, walking disaster." But then Kean is not an easy role to fill, as Derek Jacobi found when the Old Vic revived Jean-Paul Sartre's existentialist version of the old play by Alexandre Dumas *fils*. And the parallel between Kean's life and the lives of various rock stars (as reported in the press today) is surely a fair one.

But my *Globe* colleague reassured his readers that this was not necessarily the final version of the play. "With Lepage . . . you know that this interpretation is not the last and there will be, undoubtedly, new versions of the play to look forward to." Then the remarkable Lepage, after whipping up a transsexual *Macbeth* for the University of Toronto's Drama Centre in 1992, headed for the heights of Britain's National Theatre to stage a muddy *Midsummer Night's Dream*. London critics hailed him as "the Canadian whiz-kid of the avant-garde."

The remarkable Lepage is worth his space in a chapter dedicated to the eccentric genius, Edmund Kean. Lepage's theatricality is illusionistic, focusing on the visual rather than the aural. His *Tectonic Plates* and *The Visit* declared that proudly, while his University of Toronto *Macbeth* and his National Theatre *Midsummer Night's Dream* de-emphasized the language as it has rarely been, even in our most defiant Shakespearean productions. That latter work, which I saw with Garrick Hagon mud-splattered from a front row of the huge Olivier Theatre, was just about as revolutionary as Peter Brook's had been two decades earlier, being as imaginative as it was disrespectful.

Of course, we are used to producers having fun with *The Dream.* There is always the memory of Beerbohm-Tree's *Dream* with real rabbits, Granville-Barker's with gold-plated fairies, while Toronto remembers a 1954 visit to Maple Leaf Gardens which had Robert Helpmann, sequined to the eyeballs, flying across the stage with ballerina Moira Shearer .

Certainly Lepage, director of the French section of the National Arts Centre in Ottawa for a while, distinguished himself as guest director at Britain's National Theatre, as did his designer Michael Levine. Lepage's imagery is spontaneous and always fresh, but he is far from superficial. "Theatre is a vertical thing," he told *The New Yorker*'s John Lahr; "it puts us in contact with the gods, with the mind, with higher considerations." At this point in his international journeys, he was in consideration of Jean Cocteau and trumpeter Miles Davis in a very personal one man show, *Needles and Opium.*

His opera debut with Bartok's *Bluebeard's Castle* and Schoenberg's *Erwartung* for the Canadian Opera Company in 1993 was to open new worlds for him—and bring new respect for Canada's opera. In particular, I found this production of Schoenberg's solo opera to be revolutionary, as original as *The Queen of Spades* by the Czech designer Joseph Svoboda at the National Arts Centre in 1976. Lepage is certainly a major Canadian contributor to world theatre.

When his attention turns back to *Alanienouidet*, where will Robert Lepage find an actor to play Kean as our history records him? The stage's recreation of its great men of the past, Garrick to Booth to Barrymore, persists, but rarely with marked success. And when the films borrow them, only pale shadows are evoked. Yet the shade of the original Kean still haunts Old Montreal, that fiery little genius being Richard III, Othello, Shylock and Lear. To add to those famous impersonations, Kean himself took from Quebec a new role—the Huron chieftain and prince, Alanienouidet—which was to haunt him to the end of his days.

John Wilkes Booth

Born in 1838 into a leading American theatre family, third son of Junius Brutus Booth, brother of Edwin Booth. He was educated in Virginia, served in the militia and began his stage career there, then progressed to leading roles in New York, Boston, Washington, playing Hamlet, Richard III, *The Merchant of Venice*. Involved in Southern plots to abduct President Abraham Lincoln, he assassinated the President at Ford's Theatre, Washington, on April 4, 1865; two weeks later he was apprehended, shot and killed.

Beloved Assassin

The young American theatre lost a great friend and patron when Abraham Lincoln died by an act of violence on April 4, 1865. That the President died in a theatre at the hands of a member of the profession was devastating. One of the most respected players in the country, gentle Joseph Jefferson, remembered from his own days as a struggling actor the debt that theatre owed Lincoln. During a religious revival, a heavy tax on theatres was imposed. It was fought voluntarily and without fee by a young lawyer in Springfield, Illinois, whose only desire was to see fair play done. Abraham Lincoln "argued with tact, skill and humor," Jefferson wrote in his autobiography, "tracing the history of drama from the time when Thespis acted on a cart to the stage today." His good humour prevailed and the exorbitant tax was removed.

When that young Springfield lawyer rose to occupy the White House in a time of bitter national struggle, he often turned to the theatre for comfort, laughter and distraction. Lincoln loved the theatre and frequently attended, so much so that Washington audiences took little or no notice of the comings and goings of the Chief Executive. On that fatal night, the President had two invitations to theatres. He chose the comedy, *Our American Cousin* by Tom Taylor, a standby success for the actress/manager Laura Keene, which was being put on to allow for more rehearsal for *A Midsummer Night's Dream*. Arriving a little late, the President's party slipped in without interrupting the performance, although there was a smattering of applause when Miss Keene made a gesture towards the Presidential box, quickly draped for the occasion.

In the theatre all is prepared, rehearsed. Not so John Wilkes Booth's final performance in public. Frustrated in his Southern plotting, he burst into the President's box, the guard having abandoned his post to enjoy the performance, and shot him, then drew a dagger on the aide-de-camp, leapt down to the stage below, caught his spur in the bunting and broke his ankle. Flinging the motto of the state of Virginia (*Sic Semper Tyrannis*) at the unbelieving Washingtonians, he limped off in ignominy. Even that final exit was a failure, as the audience took the shot for part of the play and could not believe what it had just witnessed, "the most dastardly act an actor e'er enacted."

When the world awoke to the enormity of the crime that John Wilkes Booth had committed, it matched its grief with its fury and turned on the whole tribe of play actors. One youthful Toronto-born actress, beginning a brilliant career in Columbus, Ohio, at that time, gives a dark vision. Naturally, the theatres went dark and the managers warned the actors to avoid appearing in public. There were demonstrations in front of theatres. She herself and a fellow actress had been tacking up black cotton for the national mourning when a man shouted in their window: "They've caught the assassin. It's the actor Booth!" Knowing John, and loving him dearly, the two actresses laughed their disbelief. Then their manager, John Ellsler, came inside, perfectly white, even his lips blanched. He sank into a chair and asked, "You . . . haven't heard . . . anything?" To which they answered, "A man—he lied though—said that Wilkes Booth . . . but he did lie, didn't he?" Came the dread answer, "No. No. He did not lie. So great, so good a man destroyed and by the hand of that unhappy boy! My God, my God." And slowly he left the house. To which Clara Morris added years later: "Poor, guilty, unhappy John Wilkes Booth!"

Her remembered grief was all the greater because she had adored the young actor when he was part of the Columbus company (for players were truly itinerant in those days). She describes him vividly as "very beautiful . . . his ivory pallor, the inky black of his densely thick hair, heavy lids of his glowing eyes—were all Oriental and they gave a touch of mystery to his face when it fell into gravity. But generally there was a flash of white teeth . . . and a light in his eye. No exaggeration to say the fair sex was in love with John Wilkes Booth." Later, the little Torontonian was to play opposite Booth's distinguished older brother in his greatest role of Hamlet. Edwin retired from the stage for a while after the assassination, until he was reassured he would not be blamed.

The shock that reached across the world reached up to other Canadians—admirers, nay devotees, of John Wilkes Booth. In Montreal, especially, the assassination met with shock and disbelief, for the fiery American actor had made many friends there. Earlier, a group of Montrealers wrote inviting him to come and give them a recital at Corby Hall in St. Joseph, across the border from the U.S.A. He obliged on January 5, 1864, with selections from *Hamlet* and *The Merchant of Venice*, Tennyson's *The Charge of the Light Brigade,* and a tear-jerker called *The Remorse of the Fallen One, or Beautiful Snow.*

Accepting the invitation, the young actor replied it was his first venture into solo performance. "I have gained some little reputation as an actor, but a dramatic reading I have never attempted. I know there is a world of difference, as it is impossible to identify one's self with a single character." This confession gives a glimpse of Booth's intense involvement with a role. He has been vilified as overdramatic, but we must remember it was a period when Edmund Kean's portrayal of Shylock could make Lord Byron faint. Booth's colleagues in theatre vowed he would have surpassed the gentle Edwin in theatrical accomplishments had he lived. But where Edwin played Hamlet with romantic melancholy, John Wilkes demonstrated the Prince's madness from his first appearance.

Certainly, Montreal's Buckland management had approved him—personally and histrionically. They even brought him back, according to theatre historian Franklin Graham, for the end of the 1864 season. Booth was only too eager to come, for Montreal was a safe haven for the conspirators with whom he was plotting the abduction, rather than the assassination, of Abraham Lincoln.

According to a later historian, Edgar Andrew Collard, Booth joined his fellow Southern sympathizers at St. Lawrence Hall, Montreal's first hotel. Harry Hogan, manager of the St. James Street establishment—which was near the Theatre Royal, then on St. Paul's Street near Bonsecours—said Booth often played billiards in the basement of the hotel. Collard emphasized the fact that the twenty-six year old actor was drinking heavily at this time, suggesting that it affected his performances.

It is Hogan whom historians quote when claiming that Booth was in Montreal a week or ten days before the assassination. Hogan reported that, just before leaving town, Booth told his Montreal friends that "they would hear in a very short time of something which would startle the world." An anonymous travelling salesman wrote the Montreal papers about the dire threats that the drunken actor uttered. His friends, said Hogan, "were unable to associate the man they knew—with his gentle sympathetic ways and his quick interest in what appealed to his charity, which was as boundless as his pride—with his terrible doom." Hogan added later that "as the phantom fades away, we recollect only what was human in this rash hot-headed youth of twenty-six."

Was that "something to startle the world" assassination or abduction? There is no doubt that Booth and his fellow conspirators had plotted to seize the President at the theatre, overpower his driver, and carry him off in his own carriage to Richmond, Virginia. When that daring enterprise collapsed, the rash hot-head—unprepared and unpremeditated—plunged into what he saw as regicide, convinced that Lincoln aimed to become King of America.

Why Richmond? The youngest of the acting Booths had been born there and had begun his acting career in the South. He always upheld the Southern cause in a family of Northern sympathizers. Although "Johnnie" was his mother's favourite, nobody took the little firebrand seriously, even after he enlisted to stand guard at the hanging of John Brown when that martyr's raid to free the Southern slaves failed. Perhaps it was the need to establish his own individuality that made him so determined, for the Booths were a highly histrionic lot. Then, too, young Johnnie had to look after their father, Junius Brutus Booth, when he drank beyond control while they acted up north.

John Wilkes could hold his own on the stage, though. In November of 1864, Broadway witnessed him as Mark Antony opposite his brothers. Junius Brutus, Jr. was Cassius and Edwin was Brutus at New York's Winter

Garden Theatre. Already, Boston had acclaimed him as the most promising young actor in America. He first scored success when his loving brother Edwin sent him on as substitute to play Richard III. He soon came to play it after that occasion as "A Star of the First Magnitude" in Washington. Later, he won hearts as Romeo, Claude Melnotte in *The Lady of Lyons*, and Raphael in *The Marble Heart,* all romantic roles.

His successes are attested to by a fellow-actor, Francis Wilson, who devoted himself to "The Fact and Fiction of Lincoln's Assassination" in a book boldly titled *John Wilkes Booth.* Wilson dedicated his studious effort to "that stricken mother, Mary Holmes Booth." He was out to defy the enemies of the theatre who had conjured dire accusations against her beloved Absalom. Fortunately, he did a noble job of it. It was published by Houghton Mifflin at the Riverside Press in Cambridge in 1929, long after the wild rumors and furious denunciations had died down and the stage was seen again in its true light as an essential part of the cultural expression of those United States. Soon after that, Broadway—where the brothers had played—became an international symbol, proof that America could produce its own artists of high calibre and audiences to share their excitement.

Along with the rumors and denunciations died some of the false claims, although the puritan prejudice against play-actors never quite vanished. The testimony of Harry Hogan and of Franklin Graham was examined for inconsistency. Why didn't Graham list the late-season plays Hogan declared Booth had played in Montreal that year? Why were there no playbills or programs, asked Edgar Andrew Collard, *The Gazette's* esteemed expert on Old Montreal. In his article Collard had expressed some doubt that John Wilkes Booth ever played in Montreal; he also supported the critics who claimed that the youngest Booth was actually a bad actor, lacking the talent of his older brothers. True, Francis Wilson neglected the Canadian connection in his books, confining his investigations of the last days before the assassination to the events in Washington. But later, listing the contents of Booth's wallet—along with the photographs of several beautiful women, evidently all conquests—he mentioned "the note of exchange which Booth had bought in Montreal."

Edgar Andrew Collard was a newspaperman as well as an historian, whom we can trust to get his facts straight. But I am more theatre-man than newsman; and I tend to side with Hogan, Graham, and Francis Wilson in finding John Wilkes Booth to be the saddest, most unhappy talent who ever played upon the Montreal stage. I wind up quoting that most prejudiced, loving witness, Clara Morris: "We can only shiver and turn our thoughts from that bright light that went out in such utter darkness . . . his last words being 'Useless! Useless!'"

Mrs. Patrick Campbell

Born Stella Tanner in London in 1865. Toured Shakespeare before scoring in Pinero's *The Second Mrs. Tanqueray* (1893). Made American debut in Sundermann's *Magda* (1902); played Hedda Gabler, Electra, and Juliet, before Shaw's *Pygmalion* (1914), which was written for her, and the title role in G.B. Stern's *The Matriarch* (1929). Her correspondence with Shaw was published in 1952 and dramatized by Jerome Kilty as *Dear Liar* in 1960. She died in France in 1940.

Mrs. Pat Passes Through

Beyond any shadow of doubting, Stella Campbell—or Mrs. Pat as she was more popularly known—was the stuff of legends. Daughter of a gambling Englishman and an Italian aristocrat, she had a wit to match her beauty and an intelligence to guide her talent, even if it never guarded her tongue. To her, George Bernard Shaw lost both his head and his temper. But for her, he wrote *Caesar and Cleopatra* to play opposite Johnston Forbes-Robertson, another distinguished Victorian who lost his heart to Mrs. Pat. For her, Shaw wrote his Eliza Doolittle in *Pygmalion* and battled with her to keep it from having a happy ending. She won.

She was forty-nine when she created Shaw's flower girl in 1914, but nobody seemed to notice that. She was beautiful still, even when bedraggled, and had a voice to move angels. In fact, she could match Sarah Bernhardt in this department and did so in *Pelleas and Melisande*; or John Gielgud, for that matter, when she played Mrs. Alving to his Oswald in Ibsen's *Ghosts.* Mrs. Pat played all the great roles—Shakespeare, the Greeks. and Ibsen, as well as the new works created for her by playwrights like Shaw, Pinero and Barrie.

Mrs. Pat was sixty-nine when she passed through Montreal in 1934, en route to Hollywood. Her celebrated charms had long since faded, but the wit and eccentricity for which she was also famous had not diminished. Montreal was to get a sampling of both, as well as an echo of her theatrical gifts.

Ever in need of money, Mrs. Pat condescended to have a try at Hollywood—her second. It was a Montrealer who gave her the incentive. Norma Shearer, now the first lady of Metro-Goldwyn-Mayer Studio, was preparing a comeback after a year of nursing her husband, the MGM dictator Irving Thalberg, through an illness. Her return vehicle was to be a high-society drama about a titled woman who has an affair with another man. Shearer invited Mrs. Pat to enhance the occasion. But how was Mrs. Pat to get out to the west coast?

Other Montrealers rallied to her cause. Martha Allan, daughter of Sir Hugh Allan, head of the Allan Shipping Line and founder and prime mover of the Montreal Repertory Theatre, persuaded Sir Edward Beatty, president of the Canadian Pacific Railway, to issue a pass that would get Mrs. Pat to Hollywood. That brought her to Montreal in 1934.

Up to this point, this information has come from Margot Peters's comprehensive biography of Mrs. Pat, subtitled *The Life of Mrs. Patrick Campbell.* Now we turn to Montreal sources. It was Arthur Carveth, loyal and devoted slave of Martha Allan, whom everybody called Martha (though not to her face), who reported on Mrs. Pat's arrival. In a large hat, clutching both a mink stole and her famous little dog, Moonbeam, she sailed past Sir Edward, who had come down from his presidential office in Windsor Station to greet her. She was halfway up Windsor Street before well-wishers caught up to her and drove her to the Ritz-Carlton Hotel, the city's best and most exclusive.

Carveth also supplied an eye witness account of Mrs. Pat's visit to the Montreal Repertory Theatre. It had started off as the Montreal Theatre Guild but had to change its name to please the New York Theatre Guild if it ever wanted to stage any of the plays by Shaw, on which the NYTG had first claim. The MRT, it so happened, was rehearsing a short Shaw play, *How He Lied to Her Husband,* at the time—with Martha playing "She," Shaw's own take-off of his Candida, along with Cyril Hessey-White as her husband and Harry Donald as "He," the young man infatuated with her. It was to be played in modern dress, since Shaw was still very much alive and the fashion for playing him in period costume had not yet been adopted.

Mrs. Pat took over. In fact, in subsequent programs, she was credited officially with the direction, with Burt Hall as assistant. What a contrast between Martha, crisp and energetic with her close-cropped blonde hair, and the expansive brunette Mrs. Pat, who claimed to have created the role Martha was playing. Mrs. Pat was incandescent, if rarely technical, so she could give little help to Martha, precise and sharp-edged, whose acting was based on a technique acquired in Paris. But she did inspire Harry Donald.

Gillian Hessey-White, Cyril's daughter, is the source for her father's follow-up to that rehearsal. Happening to lunch in the Ritz-Carlton's dining room the next day, he overheard Mrs. Pat holding forth to young Harry Donald. This did not mean Hessey-White was eavesdropping, for Mrs. Pat's glorious voice was rarely muted. "My dear boy," she boomed, "you've got it all wrong!" And she proceeded to instruct the fascinated actor how "He" should be played.

There was such a marked improvement at that evening's rehearsal, Hessey-White remembered, that Martha asked young Donald what had brought it about.

"Oh, I've been giving it some thought," he replied airily to the amusement of Hessey-White, who knew full well who was responsible for the changes. Alas, in performance, Harry Donald slumped back into his old ways. But while *How He Lied to Her Husband* did not place in the second Dominion Drama Festival, Martha made history by taking home another prize—the first Sir Barry Jackson Challenge Trophy for the best play by a Canadian in the festival. Her submission, *All on a Summer's Day*, beat out Toronto's Merrill Denison and Vancouver's Alexander Ramsay.

Carveth said that Sir Edward overlooked Mrs. Pat's station snub and came through with the railroad pass. He also claimed Sir Edward gave her an extra $10,000, a massive sum in those days; but I have my doubts about that. He swore that Martha went further by taking over Loew's Theatre for a benefit concert, to which she summoned Rosa Ponselle, Lawrence Tibbett, Richard Crooks and Lily Pons from New York! Here, I think my informant went too far in proving Martha a powerhouse of generosity, especially when he claimed that he and I, the humblest of MRT workers, attended that event together.

I would prefer to remember that I attended one of the two sold-out recitals Mrs. Pat gave in the ballroom of the Ritz-Carlton. I would rather believe I sat in the gallery there and heard the great musical sound of her voice reciting from, of all things, James Barrie's *Peter Pan*. And why not? I knew my way around the Ritz-Carlton, having designed my first major setting for Ashley Duke's *The Man With a Load of Mischief*, in which that same Cyril Hessey-White played for the Montreal Repertory Theatre. Surely, nothing would have kept me away.

Well, one way or another, Mrs. Pat was helped on her

way to Hollywood by Montrealers. But her excursion there was to prove a disastrous one. Reverting to the biography by Peters, we learn that Mrs. Pat had trouble with the small part of Norma Shearer's aunt in *Riptide* and that (as a result, no doubt) she behaved with more than usual wickedness. She invariably greeted the stars of the day—Harold Lloyd, Ruth Chatterton and even Douglas Fairbanks—with "How good-looking you are; you should be in pictures!" She could not resist biting the hand that fed her. At a screening of a Shearer picture at the Thalberg home, she responded to the host's question about what she thought of his wife's performance with a famous put-down: "Oh, charming, charming. Such pretty little eyes!"

That did it. Mrs. Pat could not have worked on the set with Norma Shearer without realizing that relaxed muscles in her beautiful eyes gave her cameraman great concern. But Mrs. Pat couldn't resist the gibe. It was around this stage in the Campbell career that James Agate, the sharp-tongued British critic, remarked about Mrs. Pat: "For twenty years, she had the world at her feet and, with suicidal contempt, she kicked it away."

Her disastrous quip may not have been totally at random, but rather a judgment on that starry actress who sought to enhance her film's reputation by inviting the distinguished British actress to play a minor role in it. Sacred though Norma Shearer may have been to all the other employees of Metro-Goldwyn-Mayer, Mrs. Pat may have spotted her as a self-advancing little model of more determination than talent.

Indeed, another Britisher, Ned Sherrin, backs her up in his *Theatrical Anecdotes* (1992). He suggests that this ambitious Montrealer based her success on marrying Thalberg, thus eliciting from another MGM star, Joan

Crawford, the plaintive cry, "What chance do I have, now that Norma Shearer is sleeping with the boss?" Sherrin rather maliciously points out that Shearer made few films after Thalberg died young in 1936; after affairs with Mickey Rooney and George Raft, she married a ski instructor who was twelve years her junior.

Montreal seems to have escaped the Campbell destructiveness unscathed, save for some exchange of money. And there is a possibility that Canadian theatre might have benefitted by her presence in the past. She had been in Canada before, touring in her famous Pinero play, *The Second Mrs. Tanqueray*, in Sundermann's *Magda*, and in an undistinguished vaudeville playlet when very hard up. The latter led to another nervous breakdown, and a doctor ordered her off to the Laurentians to recuperate. She went to Ste. Agathe des Monts and enjoyed "its glorious sunsets, fields of white daisies with millions of fireflies." She also remembered that visit because there she heard of the death of Edward VII, one of her great admirers. That was all much earlier in the century, when Canada's new Governor General, Albert Henry George, Earl Grey, astonished his staff by announcing national musical and dramatic competitions, to be held annually in his name. Previously, Earl Grey had shown interest only in penal reform and sports, the latter commemorated by his presentation of the Earl Grey Cup for Rugby Football. The Grey Cup was certainly to become part of Canadian life.

It was the Toronto critic, Hector Charlesworth, a friend of Lord Grey, who gave a hint of what might have influenced the Governor General to pay attention to Canada's cultural development. Back in 1899, the fourth Earl Grey had come under Mrs. Pat's spell, having known her husband when he was an administrator in Rhodesia. The result was that he found himself becoming one of her principal backers when she went into theatre management for herself. Could this connection, his only one with the stage, have led to his surprising announcement? His Earl Grey Competitions ran for five years, building up to Lord Bessborough's Dominion Drama Festivals in 1932. May we thank Mrs. Pat for that?

ELISABETH BERGNER

Born in Austria in 1897 or 1900. Debut in Zurich as Rosalind in 1915. Later starred in Berlin, Vienna, Munich and Paris. Roles included Queen Christina and Miss Julie (Strindberg), Viola and Portia (Shakespeare), Nora (Ibsen), Saint Joan (Shaw), Marguerite Gauthier (Dumas *fils*), Nina (O'Neill). To England in 1933. Played *Escape Me Never!* (Margaret Kennedy), *The Boy David* (Barrie), *Saint Joan.* To New York in 1941. Played *The Two Mrs. Carrolls*, *Escape me Never!*, *Duchess of Malfi.* Made many films in Germany, Paris and England. Died in London, 1986.

International Gamine

The little Hutterite maid we see in the distance of the wide Manitoba landscape is indeed Elisabeth Bergner, whom I account the last of the great European actresses in the Bernhardt succession. But when the director, Michael Powell, orders his cameras into close-up, it is another kind of star we see: the young Glynis Johns. Why this substitution? What prompted this duplicity in Canada for a major British film, *The 49th Parallel*, also known as *The Invaders*?

Powell and his partner, Emeric Pressburger, came to Canada in 1941 for the preliminary shooting. Their object was propaganda, directed at American isolationism. Other major British talents had pledged themselves to the cause, including Leslie Howard, Laurence Olivier and Findlay Currie, as well as Anton Walbrook and Elisabeth Bergner. Eric Portman was cast as the Nazi crossing Canada to infiltrate its neutral neighbour to the south, with Canadian Raymond Massey as the honest fighting man who thwarts him. Most of their contributions were to be made in British studios, including that rare caricature of a patriotic French Canadian attempted by Olivier (surely his worst performance ever).

Not so the great Bergner. She joined Powell and Pressburger in Canada, in defiance of her archenemy Adolf Hitler, who had destroyed the great theatre where she made her name playing Juliet, Rosalind and Saint Joan for Max Reinhardt, as well as Ibsen's Nora and

O'Neill's Nina (in *Strange Interlude*). But Bergner decided she could not return to England to complete her scenes in close-up.

England had been good to her. It accorded her the status of immortal she had won in her native Vienna and in Germany. Under Fyodor Komisarjevsky's direction, she scored a success in *Escape Me Never!* Sir James Barrie wrote *The Boy David* for her. Shaw wrote a film scenario of *Saint Joan* for her, after she had played it at the Shaw Festival in Malvern. (He later cancelled this project, deciding it was not a role for her.) She was accepted as Rosalind despite her Viennese accent, in a film that cast a callow Olivier as her Orlando.

But the dread invasion from across the Channel now overpowered her gratitude. She knew what Nazi persecution meant, having fled from it in 1933. Leslie Howard, in his daughter's biography of him, remembered that Bergner's return to Britain was considered "unsafe." Putting the Atlantic between her and this menace, she decided to continue her career in America. She had brought *Escape Me Never!* to New York in 1935, following its London success, and won the same ecstatic response. Playgoers with longer memories recalled that *The New York Times* had once rated her Saint Joan above that of the Broadway original, Winifred Lenihan, and even over England's Sybil Thorndike, for whom Shaw wrote the play.

As was the custom for Broadway celebrities, an American tour followed New York's repeat success with *Escape Me Never!* which had chalked up a run of two seasons. And so it was that in December of 1945, Montreal had the opportunity to see the internationally acclaimed Elisabeth Bergner as the little gamine heroine of *Escape*

Me Never! The drama critic of *The Gazette* plainly fell for the skills and charms of this enchantress.

"For theatregoers there is something very exciting, evocative and a little sad to be found in the visit of Elisabeth Bergner, who has brought one of the great successes of her career in *Escape Me Never!* The play, which opened at His Majesty's last night, is the very same one that first won her rapturous audiences in London and later in New York.

"Miss Bergner is admittedly one of the great actresses of our day and perhaps the only one who can claim the title of international star. Her career has included not only the great classic roles of the famous Reinhardt productions in her native country but has also taken her all over the world and won her recognition and acclaim of a kind reserved for Bernhardt and Duse.

"To see her last night was to be reminded of those great international stars. Today, no English or American star dares venture on the stage without the comfort and support of expensive productions and fine supporting players. There is something undeniably brave in the way Miss Bergner ventures forth, unarmed save only with her great technical gifts as a player and her divine right of stardom.

"One would say that her performance of Gemma Jones in the Margaret Kennedy play has not changed in its conception one iota since it won for her that staggering ovation in London fifteen years ago. Why should it? One would not tamper with a work of art.

"She presents us with a complete portrait of the waif whose fortunes cast her in with the eccentric Sangers and make her at once victim and beloved of the most selfish of that one-time popular literary family. That odd little figure in the schoolgirl uniform entering in a flurry of temper and fright is revealed to us as a fascinating creature."

As I ran on and on, it became clear that I did not admire either her play or her supporting cast. Of the latter, I complained that "Miss Bergner has the bravado to appear in a poor company and an impoverished production." Of the former, "*Escape Me Never!* creaks in every joint, with its flubdub of mad artists, temperamental ballerinas, outraged parents and suffering in a garret." But Miss Bergner forgave me, knowing I was justified. Her fellow players could not, she informed me by phone, when I followed up an invitation to get in touch with her after opening night.

What followed was a game of intrigue, which I think the great Viennese charmer enjoyed thoroughly—a secret rendezvous with a Canadian admirer unbeknown to her fellow players. I enjoyed it equally, since I was almost as besotted as Sir James Barrie by the winsome charms, the irresistible accent, and the sharply developed theatrical judgments of Europe's greatest prewar star. She must have found my unstinting admiration acceptable, because she invited me to call on her when I was next in New York. Indeed, when she returned there, she even wired me her phone number.

"My address is 14 East 75th Street and my telephone number is Butterfield 88966 (in case I am still here when you come to New York). And may you have a happy New Year. (Signed) Elisabeth Bergner."

An invitation not to be missed. But how was I to get to New York? *The Gazette* did not, at that time, favour field trips for drama critics. I had fallen into the habit of taking my holidays where there was theatre worth writing about, and I may say that *The Gazette* never blinked when I contributed reviews of what I had seen at no cost to the paper.

The only concession was the occasional free railroad pass, an advertising perquisite then. What could justify my New York visit?

The perfect excuse soon presented itself. London's Old Vic, whose prowess under the triumvirate of Laurence Olivier, Ralph Richardson and John Burrell was already legendary, announced a season in New York's Century Theatre that coming summer. Its program—*Henry IV*, Parts One and Two, Chekhov's *Uncle Vanya* and a double bill of Sophocles' *Oedipus Rex* matched with Sheridan's *The Critic*—rang like trumpets summoning the high-minded theatregoers of America. I could not resist, and neither could some of my Montreal friends: Pierre Dagenais, director of L'Equipe; Adelaide Smith and Leo Ciceri, actors; and Don Haldane, also a director. Our excursion was made possible by the loan of an apartment on West 72nd, belonging to our friends, the Ravens. This meant we could walk home across Central Park, exulting after each show.

I played the role of knowing Broadway intimately, greeting such notables as Robert Edmund Jones and Montgomery Clift in the intermissions and slipping away to have a drink with the celebrated Bergner. But I was as awestruck as anybody.

Miss Bergner responded to my obvious excitement. She approved my delight in Richardson's superb Falstaff and in the charms of Margaret Leighton as Lady Percy and Yelena. She nodded when I recaptured the moment when this Falstaff bore Olivier as the dead Hotspur off the stage, the corpse upside-down on his back, making a memorable image of tragedy and comedy. She approved my admiration of Olivier's cool, dispassionate Astrov in the Chekhov play and my embarrassment when the Broadway audience laughed at the actors wearing their

Russian furs in one of New York's record heat waves. I saved my greatest praise for her former Orlando, Olivier, now at the peak of his powers as Sophocles' Oedipus, wrenching all hearers with his two unearthly cries when his own guilt could not be denied.

At this point, Miss Bergner interrupted. "Is this the first time you have seen *Oedipus*?" she asked. I had to admit it was, although I made some feeble excuse about my brother being taken to see Martin-Harvey in the role instead of me. "Then it is the play that affects you so much," she declared. "Larry's best performance is his Hotspur, a truly original creation."

I had to accept her judgment, for she was a keen appraiser of other people's performances. And I had to agree that Olivier's choice of a stutter over the *"W"* sound for Hotspur's roughness of speech was indeed a technical coup, leading him to the deaththroes of his last line: "Food for w-worms." But privately, I clung to my position that I had seen Olivier at his best in the role of the doomed King of Thebes: "the greatest player tested in the highest reaches of his art," as critic G. H. Lewes would insist.

I had enough tact to keep this opinion to myself when talking to the dazzling star of such popular works as *Escape Me Never!* and *The Two Mrs. Carrolls*. After all, she herself had won her reputation in the high reaches of Rosalind, Juliet, Miss Julie, *La Dame aux camélias* and Saint Joan.

She must have been rehearsing *The Duchess of Malfi* even as we spoke. Ronald Bryden suggests she was, and notes Bertolt Brecht's involvement, as Brecht's biographer, Klaus Volker, affirms; the project was a fascinating collaboration by two of Germany's most talented refugees. They had worked together before, although not too profitably for Brecht. He had been invited to update Ferdinand Bruckner's adaptation of *La Dame aux camélias* for Bergner back in Berlin in 1925; he proposed a treatment that would "bring the romantic death of Marguerite Gauthier more into line with reality and give more weight to the social elements of the plot." Volker claims that the original premise of the play "was regarded by Brecht as an ideological canard that had to be refuted."

Bergner approved and played it that way despite some reservations. When it proved unpopular, drawing antagonistic reviews, Bruckner sued the theatre, demanding that his version be reinstated. Brecht was refused his fee for his bold adaptation.

But this unhappy collaboration did not deter Bergner from working with Brecht again when they were both in New York two decades later. He had sent her his *Good Woman of Setzuan*, but she found it "as boring as it was splendid." She and her director/husband Paul Czinner wanted to follow *The Two Mrs. Carrolls* with something of a more classical nature. They agreed on John Webster's *The Duchess of Malfi* and Brecht was engaged to adapt it to the American stage. When his command of Elizabethan English faltered, W.H. Auden was brought in to touch up Brecht's revision—yet another fascinating collaborator for the German dramatist. That production opened at the Music Box Theatre in New York in October, 1946. The international charmer for whom both Shaw and Brecht wrote regained her stature as a classical actress. Briefly. Broadway remembers the occasion best because a leading black actor, Canada Lee, played in it in white-face.

After the war, Bergner did return to London to live at Number One, Eaton Square, where she resided until her death. But I never had the nerve to call on her there.

Fyodor Komisarjevsky

Born in 1882. Career as director and designer began in St. Petersburg in the theatre of his sister, Vera Komisarjevskaya. Then he had his own theatre. Later headed the Imperial and State theatres in Moscow before moving to Paris and London (1919), where he staged opera, also Chekhov, Shakespeare (at Stratford-upon-Avon) and West End drama. His American career began in 1922. Author of *Myself and the Theatre* (1930) and other books, including *The Actor's Art and the Stanislavsky System* (in Russian), *The Theatre and a Changing Civilization*, and *Settings and Costumes of the Modern Stage*, with Lee Simonson. Died in 1954.

'Cymbeline' on Mount Royal

In her account of Ottawa's Canadian Repertory Theatre, Amelia Hall reminded us that there was indeed "life before Stratford," alluding to the view of the Stratford Festival as the starting point for Canada's English-language theatre history. Even before she did, I had drawn attention in *The Globe and Mail* to the fact that all the elements which gave the Festival its success had been available in this country before, but never brought together under the commanding presence of a director like Tyrone Guthrie.

In fact, there had been plenty of productions of Shakespeare in Canada before Stratford. Even Voltaire knew that. Notable Shakespearean acting, rare revivals, modern-dress productions, Shakespearean festivals and staging, and, on at least one occasion, the participation of a visionary of world theatre—all these had been known to us.

The visionary in point was Fyodor Komisarjevsky. Before Sir Tyrone astonished Stratford audiences with his modern-dress version of *All's Well That Ends Well* in 1953, Komisarjevsky had been brought to Montreal to produce his version of *Cymbeline* atop Mount Royal. The circumstances and Komisarjevsky himself are worth recalling here.

The year was 1950, and Rosanna Seaborn Todd's Open-Air Playhouse was facing its third summer of Shakespeare. Malcolm Morley had mounted the more obvious choices in previous summers—*The Taming of the Shrew* and *As You Like It*. Now, Todd had turned her mind to something less familiar. She had chosen *Cymbeline* and had decided to play Imogen, when John Primm—successful as an actor in Canada but now working in stage management under Komisarjevsky at the New York City Opera—suggested his Russian master to the associate producer of the Open-Air Playhouse, Norma Springford. Komisarjevsky missed his Stratford-upon-Avon challenges, having done no Shakespeare in America. The result was a visit by the two Montrealers to interview Komisarjevsky in New York.

The whole venture on Mount Royal has been covered extensively by Primm, who shortly after left his post at the New York City Opera for CBS Television. After Komis's death, Primm launched a formidable biographical study of Komisarjevsky, whom he had visited in Darien, Connecticut. The production of *Cymbeline* pales as a latter-day chapter in his subject's extraordinary life; but it did put Montreal, if only momentarily, in the lead of the fashion for modern staging of Shakespeare, hitherto a costume enterprise.

Todd and Springford knew of Komisarjevsky in North America, and knew of the vast *Aida* he mounted in Molson Stadium in 1949 for the Montreal Festivals. He staged Verdi's opera with a huge folding cyclorama on which he projected the scenery. He also featured a stationary Amneris in the person of the Australia diva, Marjorie Lawrence, who was incapacitated.

Reading the publicity for that epic, Montrealers discovered some of Komisarjevsky's wide range of creativity, if only the highlights. John Primm covers the startling contrasts of this extraordinary career in full detail. He deals with the director's opposition to methods at the Moscow Art Theatre and his post-revolution position as régisseur of opera at the Theatre of the Soviet Workman's Deputies, after winning a reputation in 1906 on an experimental band-box stage. After staging *Die Walkure* and *Siegfried* in Paris in 1932, the émigré was invited, through the good offices of Serge Diaghilev himself, to stage opera for Sir Thomas Beecham in London. This he did, at the same time introducing Chekhov to British audiences at a tiny theatre in Barnes, with such young talent as John Gielgud, Jean Forbes-Robertson and Peggy Ashcroft, whom he later married. Soon after, he was upsetting staid Stratford-upon-Avon with his Shakespearean innovations.

Komis also worked in commercial theatre in the West End, directing *Musical Chairs* for Gielgud and *Escape Me Never!,* which introduced Elisabeth Bergner to London. "The most contradictory and fascinating character I have ever met in a theatre," Gielgud dubbed him, adding that he was "a real artist, a wise and brilliant teacher." Bergner's debut was so successful that she demanded Komisarjevsky direct *The Boy David,* which her adoring Sir James Barrie had written for her to play as a kind of Biblical Peter Pan. After much delay by the Austrian star, Komisarjevsky found himself in charge of an imposing assortment of personalities and talents, including C.B. Cochran as producer, Augustus John as scenic artist, William Walton for the music, as well as Godfrey Tearle and Sir John Martin-Harvey in support of Bergner. Unfortunately, *The Boy David* proved as big a disappointment as *Escape Me Never!* had been a success.

That didn't discourage the New York Theatre Guild from again inviting Komisarjevsky to New York to scale the final peaks of his career. He had staged Paul Claudel's

The Tidings Brought to Mary and Ibsen's *Peer Gynt* for the Guild; then he turned to opera again for the New York City Opera, where Primm, on a veteran-training scheme, encountered him.

Designer as well as director—he designed London's Phoenix Theatre—Komisarjevsky was incredibly versatile and always innovative. Each production had to find a new harmony with its dramatist; that was the guiding principle. When approached for *Cymbeline* in 1950, his first concern was the casting. He could accept Rosanna Seaborn Todd as Imogen, as well as Christopher Plummer and Eleanor Stuart, whom Todd also proposed; but he rejected other Montrealers of talent. He declared the eminently versatile Robert Goodier highly satisfactory as the Roman general in a black-shirt uniform. He also got along well with Bill Springford, who was responsible for lighting the open space beside Beaver Lake on Mount Royal.

The Montreal audience who climbed up Shakespeare Road was startled to find Shakespeare, even unfamiliar Shakespeare, in garden-party frocks and Fascist uniforms, and to hear snatches of American popular tunes among the couplets. The result was ahead of its time, but pleasant enough and well acted for the most part. Komisarjevsky took care to make this rare play by the bard accessible to a Canadian audience, although it was staged a good decade before Stratford, Ontario, gave it a more conventional production.

How did the Canadians respond to their legendary guest director? Were they overwhelmed by the opponent of Stanislavsky, the survivor of Meyerhold in the battle against naturalism, the Soviet Union's first opera director, the defector to the West End and Broadway, the master of vast spectacles and compact stagings of Chekhov? Were they expecting a traditionally erratic, powerful and commanding dictator of production? Very likely.

Fyodor Komisarjevsky proved to be a gentle man—slight, bald and with his very own sense of humour—who seemed more concerned with the text of this rare Shakespearean work than with the actors as individuals. Gielgud once reported that "Komis lets his actors find their way, watches, keeps silent, then places the phrasing of a scene" among their findings. I suspect that Komis found speakers of Shakespearean verse in Montreal he hadn't encountered in the United States, either in New York or New Haven where Yale University invited him to stage *The Cherry Orchard*. Many of his cast had worked for three years with the Shakespeare Society of Montreal, under the supervision of Charles Rittenhouse, who won a reputation as a director of verse in West Hill high school productions and at Yale after that. In this Open-Air cast were classical actors such as Eleanor Stuart (who played the Queen), Christopher Plummer and Robert Goodier, all of whom were later signed for major roles at the Stratford Festival.

So Komisarjevsky could afford to concentrate on that rare text, adjusting it to his modern-dress production, making it accessible to an audience who may have read it but never seen it on stage. That was a period, one must remember, when most theatres even in England concentrated on the more familiar plays, the tragedies and comedies. Komisarjevsky was discovering what Tyrone Guthrie was to find: that Canadian actors do very well with Shakespeare's "company" plays. (On this, to a great extent, rests our Stratford Festival's reputation.)

I flew from Toronto to Montreal to see the great Komisarjevsky's contribution to Shakespeare in Canada and to meet him. I had seen his productions at Stratford-upon-Avon and on Broadway. I found him to be a courteous, philosophical and theoretical person, far from demanding attention to his work. Two summers later, I went with Primm to visit his master in Darien and found a family man in a small house filled with his theatre sketches and designs, coping with his two small sons, boisterous American youngsters by then.

From Primm I learned something of the complex theories this Russian director/designer had set down—theories that Primm himself was deeply committed to bringing to the Western world. I have kept my eye on this great lifework and one summer, in a charming little chateau just thirty-five miles from Paris, where Primm and his wife Nicole live, I had the opportunity to scan Primm's manuscript, now being prepared for publication. I await a theatrical volume of unusual breadth and sweep—the biography of a master of three theatre worlds, as set down by a Canadian who has become the world authority on Fyodor Komisarjevsky.

Postscript

Komisarjevsky's opposition to Stanislavsky's methods of acting was known in Canada even before he appeared on its scene. When I followed Thomas Archer as drama critic of *The Gazette*, he gave me several valuable books on theatre (including his whole set of the work of Eugene O'Neill, a dramatist he revered more than I did). One was Komisarjevsky's *Myself and the Theatre*, published in 1930; in it, his refutation of Stanislavsky was plainly stated.

"An imaginative actor needs no naturalistic copies of the environment of his personal life to help him to act, as he is able to transform any object before him into anything he chooses to make it. . . . If it were possible for an actor to act by means of 'pure remembrance,' his rendering of a character in any play other than one written by himself for himself would be a complete distortion of the work of the playwright," he wrote. He added that each play makes its own unique demands on the player. "Shakespeare cannot be acted in the same way as Schiller, neither of these the same way as Shaw, nor can Shaw be acted as is Synge, nor Synge as is Ibsen or Strindberg, and so on."

One can only agree that this extraordinary man of the theatre makes a great deal of sense. One has only to look at the decline of theatre in New York to grasp that its resources are diminished by trying to play the classics in naturalistic terms, whereas London's theatre survives by recognizing this Komisarjevsky principle.

Elisabeth Bergner in *Escape Me Never*, in Montreal, 1945

Director and designer Fyodor Komisarjevsky in Russia, c. 1919

R.B. Ross in his maturity, c. 1917

Margaret Anglin as Medea, 1915
photo courtesy John Le Vay

Margaret Anglin

Classical actress born in Ottawa in 1876. Educated in Saint John, New Brunswick, Toronto and Sault Ste. Marie, Ontario, Sacre Coeur Convent in Montreal, and Empire Dramatic School in New York. First professional work, *Shenandoah*, for New York Academy of Music and tour; James O'Neill's Empire Company on tour; *Cyrano de Bergerac* with Richard Mansfield. Partnership with Henry Miller in *Camille* and *The Great Divide* (1901-1905). First Greek classic, *Antigone*, at Hearst Greek Theatre in Berkeley, California (1910). Later productions of *Medea*, *Iphigenia in Aulis* and *Electra*. Other plays include *Mrs. Dane's Defense*, *As You Like It*, *Antony and Cleopatra*, *Lady Windermere's Fan*, *Trial of Joan of Arc*, *Fresh Fields* and *The Woman of Bronze*. Died in Toronto in 1958.

In the Highest Realms

There is the powerful actor/manager, Richard Mansfield, at the height of his American career, interviewing a slim redhead for the important role of Roxanne in *Cyrano de Bergerac*, which he is about to introduce to North America. He condescends: "Do you think you can make yourself beautiful enough to play Roxanne?" Back comes the answer in a flash: "If you can make yourself ugly enough to play Cyrano, Mr. Mansfield!"

The great man has met his match in Margaret Anglin, despite her youth. He turns to make a remark in French to an assistant. The young lady from Canada not only supplies an answer but also corrects his French, which she speaks a great deal better than he, having been educated in convents in Montreal and Toronto. Later, she is to announce loudly, "Mr. Mansfield, you must be very careful what you say to me hereafter," after he had rather pompously chided her, complaining about the astonishing volume of her voice among other things. Margaret Anglin was a match for any actor/manager in the world.

I've always enjoyed that story about the young Canadian actress who flew so high in American theatre from that point on. I was rather astonished that her biographer, John Le Vay, attributed the first quotation to a piece about her I wrote for *The Globe Magazine* in 1957. But then, I had been collecting stories about this remarkable performer since I had first arrived in Toronto. It was frustrating that I could never meet her, for I knew she had retired to the city by then, but her family politely blocked interviews.

Is there a more exciting story in our annals than the one about the young actress who was born in the House of Commons in Ottawa —her father, the Honorable Timothy Anglin, being Speaker of that House and in residence there? Some of our great talents have been careless about their birth places; not so Margaret Anglin. Indisputably Canadian. The family had come from New Brunswick and had an Irish strain.

Convent training revealed a strong histrionic bent. By seventeen, she headed to New York, financed by her mother, herself a singer of some talent in Rideau Hall performances. A letter to August Pitou, once Sarah Bernhardt's manager, helped to win a place in the dramatic school attached to the Empire Theatre.

Now, a bare five years later, young Margaret Anglin had won the major role of Roxanne, which Bernhardt herself had created opposite Coquelin in Paris. Mansfield knew this was no role for a mere ingenue, and so did the young actress. "A most delicious *précieuse*, combining all the florid romance I am used to and all the manner I most desired to put into it," she declared.

"*Précieuse*" Rostand's heroine most certainly must be. Without her aristocratic insistence on a love as handsome as Christian and as poetically gifted as Cyrano, there is no play. Mansfield recognized that Roxanne called for high spirits, hauteur and even willfulness. Although he would rather have had a blonde in the role, he cast the Speaker's redheaded daughter from Ottawa—after keeping her waiting awhile.

Margaret Anglin made her mark that October night in 1898. "Miss Anglin flashed upon the Broadway scene like a newly discovered gem," announced The *New York Herald Tribune*. "Great as was Mansfield's triumph as Cyrano, it was also a triumph for the young unknown who played the dream-like lady of his adoration," wrote the eminent Canadian critic, Hector Charlesworth, while President McKinley's First Lady remembered the beauty of the new leading lady's performance from that prestigious first night.

How, within a few short years, had Margaret Anglin been able to match the powerful and temperamental star, Mansfield? When she spoke of "all the florid romance I am used to," she had some justification. From New York's Empire School, she had been taken by another manager, Charles Frohman, to tour in a famous melodrama called *Shenandoah*, stepping up from a small role to the lead. An audition with the king of all barnstormers, James O'Neill, brought such roles as Ophelia, Virginia in *Virginius*, and the heroines of *The Lyons Mail, Richelieu,* and *The Count of Monte Cristo* opposite the father of Eugene O'Neill. She had already served her apprenticeship and was ready for stardom.

As the comment from Mr. Charlesworth indicates, Margaret Anglin was no stranger to the Canadian public. Canada was included in the long North American tours of the day, quite profitably, and Anglin had once ventured into management herself in the Maritimes, using a student cast to support her in *As You Like It.* It was a pale introduction to her future as an actress/manager of great distinction. The enthusiastic Anglin public was situated south of the U.S. border, but Canadian admirers never lost sight of her. Nor she them.

But first, after that dazzling success as Mansfield's leading lady, she had to build her reputation as a burgeoning star. To do that, she had to be seen in the popular fare of the day, not the old familiar touring repertoire. And she had to build her own public beyond New York, which did not dominate the American scene as it did a few years later, when one read Broadway for American theatre.

The break came symbolically enough on the last day of the 19th century. Or perhaps a little later than that—the evening of December 31, 1900, according to Mr. Le Vay, poet and nephew as well as biographer. The *deus ex machina* was Henry Arthur Jones's sophisticated modern drama called *Mrs. Dane's Defence,* in which the twenty-four year old actress was seen, accepted and applauded as a woman with a past.

Mrs. Dane, according to the day's critics, proved to be the making of Margaret Anglin, winning audiences with her "peculiar quality of emotional and sympathetic appeal." As one critic explained, she had "a voice that throbs and sobs, for at the sound of it a man must weep." She herself recognized that "with the part of Mrs. Dane, my beginnings must have ended."

Her acting was also accounted as "realistic," a close imitation of nature (especially in its depths of passionate and tremulous emotion). Now she was away! Dora next, in Sardou's spy-melodrama, *Diplomacy.* (That same susceptible critic, Lewis Strang, defended himself: "She could get emotion from a keg of nails.") She displayed her versatility in *The Twin Sister*, playing both twins, of course. She showed her gift for high comedy in *The Importance of Being Earnest,* naturally playing the haughty Gwendolin. For pure sentiment, there was Pinero's *Trelawney of the Wells;* and democratically, there was a cockney social climber in another Pinero, *The Gay Lord Quex.*

Having scored in so many British imports, London managements paid some attention, especially after one of its visiting critics wrote of her: "What grace she has, what a sweet pathetic voice, what ease of movement, what absence of affectation, what genuine feeling, what moments of inspiration!" No other North American actress won such paeans from the very British Clement Scott. There were some flattering offers, the first being a chance to replace Ellen Terry in one of Henry Irving's American tours. Later both Sir Herbert Beerbohm Tree, then staging David Belasco's *The Darling of the Gods,* and Sir George Alexander, already flourishing at London's St. James Theatre, made offers. The new young star flirted with them but returned to America to rejoin Henry Miller for a grand tour of Dumas's *Camille.* Triumphant the tour was, but Anglin's Marguerite Gauthier was disliked when it reached New York. Perhaps New Yorkers still remembered the shockingly realistic consumptive that another Canadian star, Clara Morris, had given them.

By 1909, Margaret Anglin could weather such failures. Sure enough, one of her greatest hits turned up in *The Great Divide* by Frank Moody, a drama that captured the pioneering spirit of the West, then becoming one of America's last utopias. She persuaded Henry Miller to join her in it and this time the play was a smash hit in New York as well as across the country. But their joint management could not last and, with the closing down of *The Great Divide,* Margaret Anglin and her equally strong partner parted. The imperious Miss Anglin was now her own boss, as she remained for the rest of her years of stardom. Now she could do what she wanted, play where she wanted and opposite whomever she wanted.

Then what did Margaret Anglin do to enrich America's stage? She determined to bring North America the great Greek tragedies of Sophocles and Euripides, virtually unknown except in academic circles. She would play the great heroines, and on a scale to match the original presentations—in vast amphitheatres before great audiences all across America.

Anglin was remarkably persuasive on the subject of Greek tragedy, appealing to theatregoers who wanted something more than the old road melodramas or the fashionable Broadway hits. It was the Philadelphia Art Alliance, a most distinguished body, which backed the impressive staging of Sophocles' *Electra* at New York's Metropolitan Opera House, on the evening of December 16, 1917. This was no concert performance, either. One of the best of the Broadway designers, Livingston Platt, created the great bronze doors flanked by towering Doric pillars to fill the large Metropolitan Opera stage.

"The tears of old defeats are in your eyes, the trumpets of old victories are in your voice," Miss Anglin was told by critic George Sterling, thanking her for unleashing "the terror and the beauty of the past." Robert Henderson, her producer, later prepared critics and public for her by advertising, "Margaret Anglin is the greatest actress of the Greek plays in the world." The critics were convinced. The *New York Herald Tribune* exclaimed, "a magnificent performance," with the exuberant Alexander Woollcott labelling her "Anglin the Great." The critics were not merely ecstatic but seriously impressed. *The Christian Science Monitor* solemnly declared that she possessed "personal grace, emotional range and control, dignity of stature and elocutionary power."

Nor were her extraordinary performances played out

with makeshift casts of students and willing non-professionals. Not all the cast lists survive, but one from her revival of *As You Like It* in Boston around that time boasted the great road Shakespearean, Robert Bruce Mantell, as Jacques. Other notables included Louis Calhern (he survived to play Metro-Goldwyn-Mayer's title role in *Julius Caesar),* Sydney Greenstreet and Genevieve Hamper. Joining Anglin in later ventures were such acolytes as Alfred Lunt, greatly respectful of her talent as "one of the greatest stage directors and teachers of acting that I have ever known." Actually, that tribute came first from Howard Lindsay, later playwright, then stage manager, who read opposite the young Lunt when he auditioned for the great Miss Anglin.

Lunt rose to important roles in the Greek tragedies, but also toured with her in some lighter fare such as her comedy, *Beverley's Balance*, which she took to the Midwest, including Calgary, Edmonton, Saskatoon, Regina and Winnipeg, between the great Greek revivals. Other players of special note who were part of the Anglin classical repertory over the years were Clarence Derwent and Antoinette Perry, both names echoing still in awards bearing their names (Miss Perry's especially loudly when the Tony Awards are televised).

In 1915, Sophocles' *Medea* in the Gilbert Murray translation had shared the success of *Electra*. The latter was played in New York's Carnegie Hall with a famous conductor, Walter Damrosch, conducting chorus and orchestra. The even more appropriate (and impressive) setting of the University of California's Greek Theatre offered the Anglin classical company an opportunity to play a whole season of ancient Greek plays, part of a festival in conjunction with the Panama/Pacific Exposition.

Now Anglin was in her element. A cast of two hundred soldiers, attendants and supernumeraries crowded onto the stage of the Greek Theatre. A front page headline announced, "8,000 Sit In Awe As Cast Unfolds Old Greek Tale." Critic and collector of theatrical records Burns Mantle was convinced that Anglin "could do something that no other actress of her day could do." And so she could, of course. There were more heights to scale. Her special distinction in the theatre of her day won her the highest acclaim as a great actress succeeding in the loftiest realms of her art.

Today, a faded silk program heralding "The First Appearance of Margaret Anglin in *Iphigenia in Aulis*" is tucked away among the scrapbooks of the New York Library's Billy Rose Theatre Collection. So is a clipping recording that ten thousand people waited out a heavy rainstorm to see her play in St. Louis.

But it was actually her native Ottawa that gave "the Speaker's daughter" her largest audience. That was on Dominion Day, 1927, when she read Bliss Carman's ode to Canadian unity on the occasion of the Diamond Jubilee of Confederation. Her dramatic presentation drew thirty thousand people to Parliament Hill and was heard over twenty-three radio stations broadcasting across Canada and abroad. Her performance delighted her devoted friend, Prime Minister Mackenzie King, of course. The Anglin prestige was further enhanced in the nation's capital when her brother Frank was elevated to Chief Justice of Canada shortly afterward.

But even the most vibrant, melodious and emotional performer cannot dwell forever on the peaks of theatre. Although Margaret Anglin won new audiences for the Greek tragedies after the Great War of 1914-18, there had to be forays into the more frivolous popular plays to pay for her greater achievements. Time took its toll, and the period of easy drinking with her amiable young husband, Howard Hull, left her more the dowager than the lithe young heroine of the classics.

She found herself cast as the aging Mrs. Pat Campbell in a theatrical satire called *A Party*, then, replacing another Ottawa-born star, Lucille Watson, came her swan song as Fanny, the American dowager, in Lillian Hellman's war play, *Watch on the Rhine*.

It was this last role which brought her back to Canada—to the Royal Alexandra Theatre. The critics Hector Charlesworth, August Bridle and Rose Macdonald welcomed her home generously. She had long before given up her New York residence and country home in the Catskills. A few more years of strict retirement in the bosom of her family preceded the announcement of her death in a May Street nursing home on January 7, 1958.

Since I never had the chance to meet her, I can only quote the great obituary praise of others. My old mentor, S. Morgan Powell of *The Montreal Star*, reminded us that her great gift for comedy matched her high tragic range. He gave the nod to her interpretation of the witty Shakespearean heroines. But it is most likely that her ability to lighten even the darkest tragedy helped to make her "the greatest actress of her day," and a glorious name in the annals of any theatre.

Robert Baldwin Ross

Born in 1869, son of the Honourable John Ross, speaker of Canadian Senate, and Augusta Ross (née Baldwin). Educated in England and at Oxford University. Began arts journalism in Scotland in 1889. Friend and literary executor of Oscar Wilde and family. Publication of Wilde's *De Profundis* led to extended litigation with Lord Alfred Douglas. Trustee at Tate Gallery, 1917. Died in 1918, buried in Père Lachaise Cemetery in Paris.

The Dedicated Friend

Are you impressed by dedications? Do you wonder who those people are whose names or initials stand as tiny figureheads on a very large ship? Or wonder what they did to deserve such a rare honour? I will agree that our interest depends more on what is being dedicated than on the personality of the honoured party. But when the work is what is arguably the most brilliant comedy in the English language, and the dedication is to a Canadian, does not that lucky Canuck also deserve a place in this compilation?

I write about Robert Baldwin Ross, to whom Oscar Wilde dedicated The *Importance of Being Earnest* in 1895. Wilde's biographers and his own memoirs leave no doubt that "Robbie" Ross fully deserved the ennobling salutation, if only for his determined battle as Wilde's executor to restore Wilde's literary reputation, after his personal one took him to disgraceful imprisonment, decline and death.

That Ross is recognized as a Canadian may be less well established, for he was actually born in Rouen, France, and lived his adult life in England and on the Continent. Yet several factors back this proud claim for him: the distinction of his connection to the Canadian establishment of the day, his own insistence on his nationality and—perhaps most important in the world of English snobbery which he inhabited—the fact that he spoke like a Canadian all his life.

He was, with reason, proud of those Canadian connections, which gave him considerable entree into British circles. He was the son of the Honorable John Ross and his wife, Augusta Elizabeth, daughter of the Honorable Robert Baldwin, Premier of Upper Canada, Solicitor General and Attorney General (1842). The Honorable John Ross himself was Attorney General (1853) and was appointed to the Senate in 1862, where he was named Speaker. High names in a new country.

The art-loving Senator Ross took his family to France when he suffered failing health in the Canadian climate. It was there in Rouen that the youngest of his seven children was born in 1869, before the family returned to Canada at the outbreak of the Franco-Prussian War. On the Senator's death in 1871, his widow took five of the children to England, and young Robbie began his remarkable experience of English society. This included being boarded at the Tite Street home of Mr. and Mrs. Oscar Wilde and their two sons, while his mother travelled on the Continent a few years later.

The great Irish wit roguishly declared that young Robbie had seduced him when he visited him at Oxford; and the sensationalist Frank Harris spread the word that it had occurred in a public convenience (about 1886 when Wilde was thirty). That malicious, if unsubstantiated, old account persists. Novelist Robertson Davies, in *Murther and Walking Spirits*, published in 1991, enjoys the story that "a member of one of our first families" lured Wilde into "those treacherous by-paths." But the Ross biographer, Maureen Borland, backs other likelihoods. She also believes that Wilde met Ross through the Ottawa artist, Frances Richards, whom Wilde had met on his Canadian tour in 1883. Wilde thought enough of her work to introduce her to Whistler after she had exhibited at the Atelier Julien in Paris. She painted both Robbie and his brother, Alec, as well as Wilde himself. Sitting for her reportedly gave Wilde the idea for one of his best-known works, *The Picture of Dorian Gray*, making her another Canadian to influence Wilde.

Whatever the truth, if the young Ross introduced Wilde to homosexuality, it must have been rather like announcing an express train as it roared into the station, to judge from Wilde's earlier correspondence with younger men.

Whenever or whatever that first encounter, Wilde held no grudge against his so-termed seducer. Rather, he counted him as a devoted friend long past that intimacy, and indeed depended on him as the mainstay of his own stormy existence. Ross weathered with Wilde the great gale of disapproval into which he had hurled himself in full arrogance and pride. Robert Baldwin Ross fully deserved that high opinion, if only for his struggle to salvage Wilde the artist from ignominy.

Ross had started by bringing Wilde and Aubrey Beardsley together to create the illustrated edition of *Salomé* (which Wilde denied having written in French for Sarah Bernhardt) in the questionable English translation supplied by Lord Alfred Douglas. Ross contributed the preface to that version, beginning the long rivalry between Wilde's two favourites. (His preface begins, "*Salomé* has made the author's name a household word wherever the English language is not spoken.") When Wilde faced the two trials brought on by his association with Douglas, son of the brutal Marquess of Queensbury, Ross gave the greatest support, raising funds—his own and from others—and protecting the estate, which went into bankruptcy.

He remained proud of his own association, proclaiming it in the various prefaces he contributed, such as that establishing the true date of Wilde's early poem, "The Sphinx," over Wilde's less than reliable dating.

Robert Baldwin Ross fully deserved the respect of Oscar Wilde and the one honour nobody else could claim, and few could match, in the literature of the theatre—the dedication of *The Importance of Being Earnest:* "To Robert Baldwin Ross. In Appreciation and Affection." Appreciation first; affection, by then, second.

Sir George Alexander had created the role of John Worthing in his production of *The Importance of Being Earnest* at the St. James Theatre in 1895. He withdrew his production and his friendship when the Marquess of Queensbury struck Wilde down. Later, he repented enough to purchase the copyright to this great comedy. By 1910, he went so far as to revive it to mark the twentieth anniversary of his St. James's management. Furthermore, he published a limited souvenir edition of it, with Methuen and Company, the most respectable publishers of the day. He demonstrated the success of Ross's restorative efforts by inviting him to contribute a preface to this edition.

Ross had made his living managing London's Carfax Gallery, exhibiting Max Beerbohm, William Rothenstein, Roger Fry, William Orpen, and (posthumously) Aubrey Beardsley. His words in the preface remind us that he had also been an arts journalist since leaving Oxford. Having paid tribute to Alexander's revival, Ross went on to praise the actor/manager's performance of John Worthing as his "masterpiece." But in so doing, Ross admits a possible prejudice, "because the play is dedicated to myself." He continues by reminding his readers that Wilde claimed "no one particular work of an artist should be called his masterpiece, as the artist revolves in a cycle of masterpieces." In fairness, Ross then lists Alexander's other triumphs and their authors before he settles down to his own appreciation of Wilde's "trivial comedy for serious people."

"Earnest" [he uses that nickname for the play where many later admirers refer to it as "The Importance," or more familiarly just "Importance"] was the last dramatic work of its author and was produced appropriately on St. Valentine's Day. By admirers of Wilde's writings it is considered the best of all his drama, though in Germany it divides the honours with *Salomé*.

"This is not quite so incompatible as it sounds. For both plays break away from the old stage conventions and indicate that the author, always sensitive to new impressions, was absorbing what is called 'the new technique' in the modern drama. In *The Duchess of Padua*, *Lady Windermere's Fan*, *A Woman of No Importance* and *An Ideal Husband*, the older traditions are maintained. There are long speeches, asides, and 'curtains' on situations. In 'Earnest,' however, there are none of these things. The curtain descends on a frivolous observation, the frivolous situation having occurred earlier in the act.

"These were daring innovations fifteen years ago. . . . Another differentiation may be noted in the circumstance that the humour is derived from the repartee of the dialogue, hardly less than from the now classic appearance of 'John Worthing' in mourning."

This rather curious comment is more easily understood by the generation of Canadian playgoers who witnessed John Gielgud's entrance as Worthing in his 1947 tour of the play. Dressed in solid black, flourishing a black-edged handkerchief, he announced the death of his fictitious brother Earnest, when the man his ward Cicely has accepted as that sibling is present even then on the premises; certainly his announcement went hilariously beyond words, for the actor was too moved for speech. Needless to say, Wilde's dialogue was given the best possible inflection from Sir John, Robert Flemyng, Pamela Brown and Jane Baxter, while the substantial Lady Bracknell was in the hands of Margaret Rutherford, looking like a close personal friend of Queen Victoria. But that mime was, as Ross noted, on a par with Wilde's dazzlement of epigrams.

Ross goes on to term "Earnest" not only the wittiest of Wilde's plays but also the one with the fewest of his paradoxes. Then he conjures up his great friend with a quotation, not from the published writings but communicated to him personally: "There are two ways of disliking my plays: one way is to dislike them, the other is to like 'Earnest'; I shall dedicate it to you in order to prove what a bad critic you are." A typical Wildean paradox in itself.

Reverting to his honoured and honourable position as Wilde's executor, Robert Baldwin Ross finally reports that "The first holograph draft of this play, with others of the author, it has been my privilege recently to present to the Trustees of the British Museum, who have accepted them for the National Collection of Manuscripts." In doing so, those trustees of the great museum were seen to have given Wilde his proper stature as a writer of distinction. That was even more important to Ross than Alexander's revival of *The Importance of Being Earnest* a decade after Wilde's social disgrace. Alexander represented the theatre's tribute, but the British Museum the respect of the nation.

The Importance of Being Earnest has survived to find a very special place in world theatre, outliving a scandal that was more than a parochial one. That a Canadian played a large role in bringing Wilde's recognition as a true artist seems a matter for some pride, and full justification for Robert Baldwin Ross's inclusion in this book.

Mary Pickford

First international film star. Born in 1893 in Toronto. First professional appearances in Toronto stock companies in 1899. Broadway stardom in *The Warrens of Virginia* in 1907. First films in 1909. Later starred in *The Poor Little Rich Girl*, *Rebecca of Sunnybrook Farm*, *Daddy Longlegs*, *Little Lord Fauntleroy*, *Sparrows* and *Coquette*. Second ever winner of an Oscar for acting. Formed United Artists in 1919 with her husband Douglas Fairbanks, Charles Chaplin and David Wark Griffiths. Died in Hollywood in 1979.

Our Mary as Cleopatra

Mary Pickford as Cleopatra? "America's Sweetheart"—one of our home-grown talents—cast as the Serpent of the Nile? Such a seemingly ridiculous flight of fanciful casting was enough to send me to the British Film Institute to check out the truth.

That afternoon in London, I discovered that Mary Pickford indeed had been quite serious about playing Egypt's Queen, but that she had been frustrated by one of the world's greatest dramatists—a man even more Irish than she was—George Bernard Shaw. It was a battle of Titans: a confrontation between the first world-famous film star and the wily world dramatist.

Mary Pickford had been a favourite of mine since I first saw her in films. I responded to her as a child, more directly than I did to those other great film pioneers—her friends Lillian Gish and Charles Chaplin—who both embarrassed me for some reason. Not Our Mary, though: she was resolute, resourceful, sunny and funny.

Later, I respected her as a strong force in motion pictures, as a woman who had won the largest audience in the world, because her subtitled films could be shown everywhere. And also because she was the artist in control, running United Artists for her two founding partners, Chaplin and her then-husband, Douglas Fairbanks. That she was also a Canadian didn't concern me so much at that time.

Mrs. Pat Campbell as
Eliza Doolittle, 1913

Mary Pickford in 1927 film
My Best Girl

George Bernard
Shaw on film set,
1945

Beatrice Lillie, 1933
Whittaker caricature

Later on, I became aware that Mary Pickford learned her lifelong trade of child actress in Toronto's stock and touring theatres, winning her first audiences there. Gladys Smith, as she was born, was five when a stage manager who boarded at her mother's house on University Avenue suggested that the little girl might be able to play the part of Ned Denver in a contemporary melodrama, *The Silver King*. Which she did, managing to steal several scenes. Her earnings became very useful to the Smith household after her father, John Charles Smith, died, and soon little Gladys, despite her youth, was a regular and recognizable player on the local scene. Her first production photo from 1899 or 1900 lists her as playing in *The Silver King* at age seven.

Despite her vague memory for dates, Mary Pickford remembered loving the sad scene as Little Willy in *East Lynne*, going to heaven as Little Eva in *Uncle Tom's Cabin*, and playing a dying consumptive boy in a play called *The Sudan*. She even played vaudeville, dressed in a fairy costume and passed from one actor's arms to another in *The Littlest Girl* (a one act play). Robert Windeler, her 1974 biographer, omitted mentioning that one of the tall actors who hoisted "Baby Gladys" onto his shoulder for the curtain call was a young Torontonian then named Walter Houghston; later, he founded a film dynasty as Walter Huston, after stardom on Broadway and in Hollywood.

"Baby Gladys" soon won billing and local stardom in several Toronto stock companies, including the high-ranked Velentine's Stock Company. Not all the Pickford training was acquired in her home town, but certainly enough to attract outside attention. When she and the rest of the acting Smiths—Mother, Lottie and little Jack—appeared in Hal Reid's new comedy, *The Little Red Schoolhouse* (Windeler sets this at 1901), the playwright was so impressed that he promised them all the New York opening. Mrs. Smith immediately sold the Toronto house. Alas, the rights to the play went elsewhere, and Lillian Gish was hired for the pre-Broadway tour. But luck was with the Smiths, if not the Gishes, and Lillian had to return to New York. Sent a telegram offering little Gladys the role, Mrs. Pickford wired back an ultimatum: all the Smiths or none. She won, and Baby Gladys and family were Broadway-bound.

Next, they were on stage with the dashing Chauncey Olcott in a historical play, *Edmund Burke*, which took them through 1905-06 with its Broadway run and long strenuous tour. By 1907, after some film dalliance, Gladys Smith was back to invade the great David Belasco's office and win a lead in his latest epic, *The Warrens of Virginia*, by William C. de Mille (the famous director's older brother).

But the name "Gladys Smith" was insufficiently dignified for Belasco. She suggested "Pickford" and hoped for "Marie." He settled on "Mary Pickford." And so it was from then on—in *Seven Sisters* with Laurette Taylor and in *The Good Little Devil* with Ernest Truex. For that, Mary earned twenty-five dollars a week. She changed it all to one dollar bills to make it seem more. More money was always a major interest to this little Canadian.

Mary Pickford retained her Canadian connections all her life. When I talked to her at Pickfair, the Fairbanks/Pickford mansion, near the end of her career, she had vivid memories of growing up in Toronto: of being left in her baby carriage outside Eaton's department store, of tobogganing on University Avenue where the Hospital for Sick Children now stands.

She had, over the years, made many triumphal returns to her native soil. Because I was a fan of such long standing, I managed to attend a press conference at the old Windsor Hotel in Montreal when my childhood idol made one of her state visits. I was a junior on *The Gazette,* but uttered not a word during the interview, so much in awe was I. I was grateful when one of the women reporters, gushing a little, confessed that she had never forgotten that moment in *Sparrows* when Miss Pickford realized that Jesus had come to take the child dying in her arms. Miss Pickford was persuaded to enact the little scene for us.

It was amazing. By then the famous child actress was well into her forties or beyond; still charming, still pretty, but obviously no child. Yet, as she demonstrated her gift for pantomime (as early motion-picture acting was), the scene came alive in all its pathos. The love for the imaginary child, the recognition of the vision before her, the realization that the child in her arms was dead—all were clearly demonstrated, and held the roomful of reporters in silence. We were all aware that we were witnessing a world-renowned artist in performance.

Then, with a spark of her famous spunkiness, Mary Pickford dealt with the question of age. She told us that she was sick and tired of having elderly gentlemen tottering up to her swearing that their mothers had taken them as tiny children to see her. She had been a child in films for so long that people became confused about age—hers and their own. By then, Pickford had given up trying to find adult roles in which her public would accept her. With talkies, she had made the jump to show that she could act grown-ups too. Indeed she could: her first talking film, *Coquette*, won her the second Oscar ever given.

An earlier role, as a Spanish gypsy in *Rosita*, directed by Ernst Lubitsch, was a failure with the public, while the first Shakespearean play filmed as a talkie, *The Taming of the Shrew*, won more credit for its "added dialogue by Sam Taylor" than as a classic film.

It must have been around this time that Mary Pickford started negotiations to play the young Queen of Egypt in George Bernard Shaw's *Caesar and Cleopatra*. This was the venture which caught my fancy that time in London. The incident might have been brought to my attention by something Michael Holroyd, Shaw's biographer, said to me when he was researching the productions of Shaw in Canada.

Hollywood had long been dancing attendance on Shaw, even before talking pictures were unleashed. One of Hollywood's blandishments had given birth to a famous Shavian paradox. Speaking to Samuel Goldwyn, Shaw declared: "The trouble with you, Mr. Goldwyn, is that you're only interested in art, while I'm only interested in money." But there is no doubt that Shaw was interested in motion pictures as a means of extending his public as well as his income. The text of *Caesar and Cleopatra* (1899) betrays his dalliance, with scene changes described in cinematic rather than stage terms. What made him reject later offers was the belief that Hollywood's scenario writers would play havoc with the Shavian texts in making their adjustments to the camera.

Shaw's interest in films was intensified in the late

twenties when the silent screen found its tongue. The Theatre Guild had staged *Caesar and Cleopatra* in New York in 1925, with Helen Hayes as the young Queen. In the audience was the vivid Polish actress, Pola Negri. Being a siren by profession, Miss Negri immediately saw herself playing Cleopatra in a film spectacle, and proceeded to London to vamp the great dramatist into giving her the rights. She managed to get herself invited to lunch at Shaw's apartment.

Emerging from that meeting, she confided to the world press that she had been successful in her quest. Even *The New York Times* swallowed her story, reporting: "Pola Negri has come, seen and conferred with GBS. Emerging triumphantly from a lunch . . . she announced that, the first time a Shavian play is to be screened, it will be *Caesar and Cleopatra* and that she will play Cleopatra. . . . Apparently, what all of Hollywood's aureate allurements could not accomplish has been achieved by the wit and perhaps the charm of a woman. Not only did Shaw consent to release his play, but he made the even more astounding concession that he might alter it to suit the film." The story added, "Pola Negri could scarcely talk under the strain of excitement when she returned to her hotel. 'Such a g-r-r-reat man!' she exclaimed."

But just who had been charmed and who had been in full control of that encounter with the latest emissary from Hollywood emerged much later when Shaw's secretary, Blanche Patch, revealed that he had been having a little fun at Pola Negri's expense, while also sending out a message to future negotiators. Miss Patch had typed a paragraph from Shaw's shorthand, addressed anonymously to *The Daily Mail*. It read: "It is an open secret that Pola

Negri saw great screen possibilities in *Caesar and Cleopatra* when it was produced by the Theater Guild in New York three years ago. It is equally well known that Mr. Shaw's plays have been dismissed so often by the critics as 'all talk' that he has confessed to an impish desire to see his plays with the talk omitted. On other grounds, too, Mr. Shaw is known to be a movie fan. Therefore, though the official report is that nothing has been settled, it seems not impossible that Pola Negri's hurried visit to London will not have been in vain." Was Shaw aware then that the talkies were imminent? Of course he was.

What the mischievous Irish genius did not mention was that, when his child Cleopatra came to the screen, if ever it did, she would not be presented as a mature and black-browed vamp like Pola Negri. Shaw had been dismayed long before by Mrs. Patrick Campbell's interpretation of Cleopatra as a mature siren, when she had obliged him by reading the part in a "performance" to establish copyright (Sir Johnston Forbes-Robertson reading Caesar). Shaw did approve the Theater Guild's choice of Helen Hayes and Sir Johnston's wife, Gertrude Elliott, in the London premiere. But he was adamant that his heroine was the young Cleopatra, not a rival to Shakespeare's Queen of Egypt.

So, when Mary Pickford came to Ayot St. Lawrence, Shaw used a different approach to that with which he had teased Pola Negri. He admittedly accounted her a "temptress" when she asked for the rights to make a talking version of the play. She countered by pointing out that, of all Hollywood stars, she had the greatest experience in interpreting adolescents, which he could not deny.

(She was also interested in *The Devil's Disciple* and *The Showing-up of Blanco Posnet.*)

As an actress and "temptress," America's Sweetheart might well have persuaded Shaw, interested as he was in filming his plays if given some guarantee of studio respect for the original text. Pickford still had her youthful, even childlike, good looks and great charm. And as she said at the time, "Mr. Shaw is most insistent in the play that Cleopatra is only a young girl just starting in her teens. Well, I am the only actress in Hollywood who is capable of playing a really young girl and also accustomed to acting as a queen." As a film fan, Shaw must have agreed that she could still play youngsters if he saw her 1928 comedy, *My Best Girl.*

But it was Mary Pickford the dominant producer of United Artists who put him on guard, or rather, kept him on guard. She insisted on a specially written scenario of *Caesar and Cleopatra*, and obviously was not going to invite Shaw to provide it, inexperienced as he was as a scriptwriter. That did it, according to a respected study called *The Serpent's Eye: Shaw and the Cinema.* According to that exploration of the long flirtation between Shaw and Hollywood, the dramatist finally demanded of Miss Pickford: "Is the play not good enough? I am waiting until the talkies are through with scenarios and are ready for me as I am." (He held out until 1938 when that persuasive Hungarian Gabriel Pascal convinced him he would be in strict charge of the screen adaptation of *Pygmalion.*)

That ended the dream of seeing Our Mary play Cleopatra. Despite the undeniable charm and Egyptian kittenishness of Vivien Leigh in the role when *Caesar and*

Cleopatra finally came to the screen in 1945, I still regret that we didn't see the cinema's most famous "child," perched roguishly on the Sphinx with Julius Caesar, ply her Irish charms on him. That would have been one for the British Film Institute, and a gem for collectors of historic video classics.

BEATRICE LILLIE

Comedienne, born in Toronto in 1896. She trained in concerts throughout Ontario before sailing for England in 1914. Debut at Chatham Music Hall in 1914, London debut same year in Charlot revue, *Not Likely*. Broadway debut in Charlot's *Review of 1924*. Married Robert Peel (later Sir Robert) in 1920. Starred in New York and London in many revues, musical comedies, cabarets and vaudevilles; also films and troop shows between 1939 and 1946. Retired in 1967; died in England in 1989.

The Kid from the Canadian Sticks

When the world swung full circle from an age of Victorian innocence towards the knowing sophistication that followed World War I, it is interesting to note that the City of Toronto obligingly provided icons for each phase. Mary Pickford and Beatrice Lillie were the two successful and legendary extremes.

How did this then unexciting city on the shores of Lake Ontario muster the background, the ambiance and the training to produce such an impressive pair of opposites? A good question, I think. Especially when you discover the similarities of their backgrounds.

Both were born at the end of the Victorian era, within three years of each other; each had a rather ineffectual father matched with a resourceful and ambitious mother. One difference: Pickford's mother was Irish, Lillie's English/Spanish. They shared the same lower middle-class background and knew the nudge of poverty. Neither had much schooling, although at one time both attended Gladstone Road School.

Both women were personalities uniquely suited to the changing day—fascinating and quick-witted enough to meet the requirements of early motion pictures or post-war London revues. That each had the mother of all stage mothers supplies the motivating force, but Toronto may be allowed more than a little credit for providing opportunities for their rising talents. Both learned their trade at home before setting off to exploit it and win world fame.

Where the precocious Pickford found her first steps on the fast ladder in local stock theatres, Lillie's escape route was more torturously taken through church basements and church choirs, then on through a wide provincial concert circuit. Perhaps I have not given Charlotte Pickford full credit in my reporting on her amazing offspring, but it is inescapable in the case of Mrs. Lillie. She herself was the star of The Lillie Trio, "high-class entertainment," when it went on ever-widening circuits of Ontario communities from North Bay to Niagara Falls, including Sturgeon Falls, Elk Lake, Cobourg, and Cobalt. When they played Shea's Hippodrome in Toronto, the trio merged with The Belles of New York.

Lucie Lillie was the star soloist, with the gifted Muriel a good second as the pianist. Muriel won an Earl Grey Music and Dramatic Competition; Little Bea was thrown out of the Cooke Presbyterian choir for making people laugh.

Undaunted by impending war, Mrs. Lillie decided that Muriel should have her proper chance, and so should she herself. They sailed for England in 1914; Bea followed shortly afterward, by herself. She was then eighteen, a bit too young to be trailing around for auditions as a singer. But one desperate rendition of "God Save the King" got her into a chorus, after some attempts in music hall. Actually, the war helped Bea Lillie, for the chorus men of England had enlisted, and there was a place for a boyish little Canadian. In fact, in her first appearance in England at the Chatham Music Hall, she was dressed as a

Canadian Tommy singing about missing his mother.

In the London chorus line, she was often put into white tie and tails. It was in this natty garb that she gave vent to Muriel Lillie's composition, "Oh, take me back to the Land of Promise." In the land of ice and snow, Muriel believed, "down lover's lane, where the maple leaves grow, skating, baseball and canoeing," is the place to do your billing and cooing. Serious tribute to their Canadian allies, the British could take; but when Beatrice Lillie progressed to "Bird of Love Divine" in a piercing soprano, they couldn't help laughing. Neither could Noel Coward, AWOL from barracks. It was his first glimpse of Lillie's potential as a sendup comedienne.

Fortunately, the man who was in a position to use such a rare singing comedienne was on the scene—a French entrepreneur named André Charlot, whose revues were already catching Londoners' fancy. That chorus job she won with the national anthem was in a Charlot line in a show called *Not Likely,* to be followed by *The Nine O'Clock Revue.* When her rendition of "We're drifting apart, You're breaking my heart" failed to move him, she tried a little satirical travesty; and Charlot hired her from then on as a comedienne.

Coward wasn't so lucky when the "kid from the Canadian sticks" (her own description) tried to get him an audition with Charlot. His side-kick, Gertie Lawrence, did better and wound up as Bea's understudy, later her co-star and constant partner in whatever mad pranks they thought they could get away with. In no time, the pair were the toast of London town. They were regulars at the Fifty-Fifty Club on Wardour Street, in which Ivor Novello had money. Novello, the reigning matinee idol of the day and immensely talented as a musician, kept a flat under the dome of the Aldwych Theatre. That was the true gathering place of smart London, including Gerald Du Maurier, Gladys Cooper, Charles Cochran, Lily Elsie and the stage-door johnnies in uniform, including the dashing Prince of Wales. Novello was working at the Air Ministry in Whitehall, so a short dash down to the Strand allowed him to greet the theatre set. Yes, there were bombs and air raids, but Novello's friends defied "the Huns."

Incidentally, Novello retained Lillie's affection and admiration, which Noel Coward did not always do. Although Coward wrote some of her very best material, including "Mad Dogs and Englishmen"' they fought when working together. The Lillie genius for comedy did not respond easily to other people's direction.

But the astute Frenchman Charlot, knew how to use this unusual talent. He starred her with the dapper Scot, Jack Buchanan, in his *Review of 1924,* then whisked them off to Broadway, with Gertrude Lawrence also promoted to lights. Until then, audiences were used to the grand "girls, girls, girls" shows of Flo Ziegfeld. But Charlot's dependence on nothing but smart lines and smarter performers caused a bit of a revolution on the Great White Way. Indeed, at one point on their last night, Bea and Gertie were driven along Broadway, sitting on top of a limousine—a new version of the carriage horses of earlier stars.

So now, the kid from the Canadian sticks was the toast of another show town. She was even more an oddity there, because she had been courted and won by a scion of Britain's solid nobility, Robert Peel of Drayton Manor. He included a prime minister and the founder of London's police force among his ancestry, but was himself a rather feckless gambler once out of the war. Thus their posh country wedding did not appreciably interrupt the Lillie career, as the money was needed to keep Robert in the style in which he had been raised, and to raise their son, Bobbie, in a different but similar style.

A tragedy lay behind Lillie's scintillating career. Sir Robert Peel drifted away, and Lady Peel was left to raise Bobbie with help from her mother and sister. The bright, handsome boy volunteered as an able seaman in World War II and was reported missing off Ceylon in 1942. Mrs. Lillie withheld the Royal Navy letter confirming his death, because Bea Lillie was just opening again in New York. It took sad years of hoping before she was to learn by accident that the son who was the love of her life was really dead.

During the years between the wars, Beatrice Lillie's transatlantic career was at its highest point. The *Review of 1924* was followed by *She's My Baby* and *This Year of Grace*, which Coward had written and composed for her. By then, the rest of the American continent clamoured to see the bright Britishers in their bright little revues. As the shows travelled, of course, their casts tended to be whittled away due to previous engagements. By the time *This Year of Grace* hit Montreal's His Majesty's Theatre, Beatrice Lillie was its sole star. So she got to sing all the hit numbers—"World Weary," "A Room With a View," "Mad About the Boy," "March With Me"—and was somehow involved with the masked ballet, "Dance, Dance, Dance, Little Lady."

That couldn't have suited this Outremont schoolboy better; I was absolutely astonished by the Lillie comedy style, as well as by her material. For me, as for so many North Americans, here was a brand-new sophistication, all cheerful innuendo and sly comment.

I learned to raise one eyebrow and adopt an air of world-weariness, which must have puzzled my Strathcona Academy teachers. (The American revue that had a similar effect on me came much later—Irving Berlin's *As Thousands Cheer*, which was much more elaborate when seen in New York). What *This Year of Grace* was inventing for us was a new kind of send-up of everything in sight—as much "put-down" as "send-up," something that later turned into "camp." Certainly Beatrice Lillie was mistress of the genre, and never more so than when marching back and forth across the stage as Britannia, singing "March, March, April, May and June/Canada! Australia! South Africa!/ To merely name a few." But she was not just "camp"; she could summon pathos, as she did in "Mad About the Boy," evoking the hopeless passion for a favourite film star. So there was a range with this new knowingness.

From that time on, Beatrice Lillie's activity was prodigious, even frenetic, with revue following revue, an occasional film, vaudeville and musical comedy following without interruption. In London, she headed the bills at The Palladium and Café de Paris; in New York at the Palace Theatre. She played in thirty revues and a dozen musical comedies. She starred in the golden jubilee of the *Ziegfield Follies* and won all hearts as a mermaid in *Inside U.S.A.* Noel Coward wrote "Marvelous Party" for her; Cole Porter, "Mrs. Lowsbrough-Goodby." She made *Auntie Mame* her own back in London, and was in the world premiere of a Shaw fantasy, *Too True to be Good*, for the New York Theater Guild (not a successful venture for her). Matching all this was her hectic social life, which brought her together with all the names of the day—from Tallulah Bankhead to Fanny Brice, to the wits of the Algonquin Round Table, and film stars from Garbo to Gable.

To make the going physically harder, she did another lot of troop shows, working under quite desperate conditions to cheer the boys abroad. Prince Philip of Greece was a schoolmate of her son Bobbie, and often slept on the sofa in her London flat before making his royal alliance. When Toronto decided to put up a plaque to its extraordinary native daughter, the Duke of Edinburgh unveiled the tablet. He never revealed how well he had known her personally, instead stressing the importance of her entertaining of British troops.

Her last real hit was *An Evening With Beatrice Lillie.* This was almost a one woman show, and so could and did tour extensively. A moment at the end of the first act caught the extraordinary rapport she could achieve with her audience. Act One found her listening intently to John Philip Huck as he sang "Come into the Garden, Maude" to her, then led her offstage as the curtain fell. Act Two opened with a startled Bea Lillie entering, looking back offstage. Then she turned to us, exclaiming, "I thought he was with you!" The whole house exploded with laughter.

An example of how she made everything over in her own way came in her performance in *High Spirits*, Broadway's 1964 musical version of Coward's successful *Blithe Spirit.* As immortalized by Margaret Rutherford, Madame Arcati was a bumbling innocent in the field of spiritualism. Not so Bea Lillie. The part grew as she fought for more songs. It also changed from night to night. Tammy Grimes, who was featured in it, reported that Auntie Bea never went after the same laugh twice in succession, so confident was she in her ability to raise other laughter. We got a glimpse of what Lillie's Arcati must have been like when Tammy, who had played Elvira in the musical version, came to Niagara-on-the-Lake to play Arcati herself in Coward's play. Gone was the original victim of the hero's snide jokes. Instead, Arcati was now a faddy but superior eccentric, putting her host down. Not a figure of other people's fun. No wonder there had been battles backstage between Lillie and Coward, who had directed *High Spirits*.

By mid century, the astonishing Lillie career was on the wane. People still cherished memories of her opposite another zany, Bobby Clark, in *Walk a Little Faster*, or Bert Lahr in *At Home Abroad*, and, especially, of her swinging out over the audience in *The Show Is On*, sitting on a moon tossing out garters. But these were all thirties triumphs. More recent audiences tended to recall her in films—the 1948 *Dr. Rhythm* with Bing Crosby, or *Thoroughly Modern Millie*. Helen Hayes, in a 1974 interview, asked, "Did you know that Nancy Hamilton once wrote a musical about Mary Poppins? For Bea Lillie? For a while, Billy Rose was going to put it on." Instead, *Mary Poppins*, the flying governess, emerged years later as a film starring Julie Andrews. Andrews also starred in *Thoroughly Modern Millie*, Beatrice Lillie's last film. It captures some of the rare Lillie persona, and she is delightful in her scenes with Andrews. But in the studio, she had difficulty remembering who she was.

The year she filmed *Thoroughly Modern Millie*, 1967,

was the year Canada saw its last of its most famous eccentric. Bea Lillie shared a double bill with the little-known singer, Julio Iglesias, at the big O'Keefe Centre, new since she had visited ten years before. Her first night was a happy homecoming, with Mrs. E.P. "Winnie" Taylor greeting her old friend. But attendance fell off, according to O'Keefe's manager and historian, Hugh Walker, as new audiences found her famous material dated or too camp. Walker labeled her 1967 visit an unsuccessful attempt at a comeback.

When audiences did not roll about at the wickedness of "Rotten to the Core, Maude," or "Wind Round My Heart," or even "There Are Fairies at the Bottom of Our Garden," it was obvious that the sophistication Bea Lillie had introduced had not stopped with her but had gone on to more cynical expression. Sadly but truly, the Lillie wit was losing some of its sharpness. Ken Tynan, in a celebrated interview in *The New Yorker*, pinned her down: "She is uniquely alone. The audience, like Alice, is just a thing in her dream." In private life, she became more eccentric. A personal appearance at the Museum of Modern Art in New York, which was showing one of her films, found her attempting a strip tease—and not as a comedy act.

Helen Hayes remembered, "The last time I saw her was when I was playing in *Harvey* with Jimmy Stewart, which would be 1970. She came backstage with John Philip. There were a lot of other people there so I leapt up to give her my seat at the dressing table. She sat down, looked at herself in the mirror and said: 'I don't like this face, bring me another one!' The next minute she was gone. Didn't know who I was. She was never quite of this world." Helen Hayes, the sanest of actresses, hit on the basic quality of the clown, as had Tynan: a being not of this world, yet in it, who makes a commentary on it.

Finally, in 1975 came the stroke that left her speechless, nearly blind. Where was she to live out the rest of her life? Was it to be at her house in Connecticut? The flat Helen Hayes had found for her in New York? Certainly not the stately home of Lady Peel, Dayton Manor in Staffordshire, long since sold off. She had once bought a comfortable home in Henley-on-Thames, almost by accident, and it was to this retreat she was taken, looked after by the faithful John Philip Huck, her devoted companion since they had met during *Inside U.S.A.*

A sad auction of her memorabilia, dating back to her beginnings in Canada, was held a year after her death. The material had been assembled by John Philip during her last years, but he was not on hand to see the sale; he died the day after his beloved star, the kid from the Canadian sticks.

When Bea Lillie died, Sir John Gielgud, who had done army tours with this extraordinary comedienne, was asked to contribute a memorial notice. He did, quoting critic Kenneth Tynan's perceptive magazine profile of Bea Lillie: "The fact that we are amused proves that she has conquered the rarest of all theatrical arts, the art of public solitude, which Stanislavsky said was the key to all great acting. To carry it off, as she does, requires a vast amount of sheer nerve and more than a whiff of genius, which is another word for creative self-sufficiency. One might add that it probably helps to have an experience, at an early age, of pulling faces in a church."

The kid from Toronto would have undoubtedly

responded to this with a campy, "Get *him*!" Lady Peel would have felt much more at home with the label supplied by her old sparring partner, Noel Coward, that impudent cockney turned guru, when he conferred upon her the definitive title, "The funniest woman in the world."

Christopher Plummer

Star of stage, screen, television, and whatever next, born in Toronto in 1927. Moved to Montreal and began his acting at Montreal High School, then at Montreal Repertory Theatre and the Open-Air Playhouse. Professional debut at Stage Society and Canadian Repertory Theatre, both in Ottawa. Summer stock followed and his New York debut came in *The Starcross Story* (1954), followed by the American Shakespeare Festival (1955) and the Stratford Festival, Ontario (1956). London debut in *Becket* (1962). Films began in 1956 and include *Fall of the Roman Empire*, *The Sound of Music*, *The Man Who Would Be King*. Television (beginning in 1953) includes *Oedipus Rex*, *Hamlet at Elsinore*, *Cyrano de Bergerac*, *Macbeth* and *Counterstrike*.

The Gentleman Player

"Tennis anyone?"

That creaky old line of dialogue introduces one of Canada's most successful actors, a "star of stage, screen and television." Christopher Plummer has always been insouciant, debonair, to the manor born. And he plays a good game of tennis.

That counted. When that old master of the doubletake, Edward Everett Horton, toured André Roussin's farce, *Nina*, in the fifties, he was looking for a competent juvenile actor who also played a good game of tennis, since that was Horton's way of keeping in trim. Young Plummer from Senneville, Quebec, filled the bill admirably, and could also behave as a gentleman-player should.

I have an earlier memory or two of young Plummer, having reviewed him as Darcy in *Pride and Prejudice* at the Montreal High School. I was astonished that any student had the manner, the diction, the hauteur of Jane Austen's snotty hero. Doreen Lewis, who left teaching at the school to run the Montreal Repertory Theatre, once told me how Christopher had commandeered the piano in the school gymnasium. From the shadow of the balcony, his voice rang out as if he were a school official: "All right, you kids. Out of here!" That trick left the keyboard to himself. He was, and is, a gifted musician—a plus in his acting career, too.

When Malcolm Morley directed Sheridan's *The Rivals* for Brae Manor's summer theatre in Knowlton, Quebec, the French Canadian student who was to play Faulkland found the text too much for him. They called Montreal to fetch young Plummer, who learned the role during the drive out. Or most of it. When he forgot a line during performance, he turned to the prompt girl and asked politely, "What's the line, dear?" As Brae Manor legend has it, she fainted.

That impressed Morley, then scouting for Ottawa's Stage Company, precursor to the Canadian Repertory Theatre. There the teenaged Plummer, who had gone from playing high school Austen to Shakespeare at the Open-Air Playhouse to Sheridan at Brae Manor, was introduced to the rigours of weekly stock performances. In his years in Ottawa (with a side-season in Bermuda), he became immensely versatile, always playing above his own age. Off-stage he remained a teenager, enraging Morley, who found him unreliable, irresponsible and untidy. Such an off-stage judgment kept him out of Tyrone Guthrie's first Stratford Festival company. I assured Dr. Guthrie that he himself would have no trouble keeping Chris in order, but other advisors warned that Plummer was intractable.

A ladies' man from an early age, young Plummer naturally antagonized other males—another factor that helped to block him from Stratford. Amelia Hall was greatly annoyed by this wayward youth's behaviour backstage, but she did appreciate his acting talent when he joined her beloved Canadian Repertory Theatre (CRT). He played a startling range of parts, most of them beyond your average nineteen year old. He showed his special talent as the aging Crocker-Harris in *The Browning Version*, embittered Tom in *The Glass Menagerie* and old Dr. MacPhail in *Rain*. He was soon a great favourite on the boards in Ottawa, if not backstage, standing out in a company that later included William Hutt, Donald Davis, Ted Follows, Richard Easton and William Shatner.

The CRT bridged the winter months for these bright beginners, who had honed their skills on CBC radio drama, in summer stock, and in the Dominion Drama Festival. It was in summer stock that young Plummer joined the service of the itinerant Edward Everett Horton as supporting juvenile and tennis partner. His on-court expertise kept him on tour for the rest of the summer, then pointed him in the direction of Broadway. He lists *The Starcross Story* as his New York debut in 1954. Next he moved to *Home Is the Hero* and then joined America's First Lady of the stage, Katharine Cornell, and Tyrone Power in Christopher Fry's *The Dark Is Light Enough.*

In the latter, he caught the eye of Raymond Massey, who wrote: "One young actor who played a Cossack . . . had only a few lines, no movement, but he could listen. During the scene, neither of us [Denis Carey, the English director] could take our eyes off him in spite of the competition from two of the most expert eye-catchers in the business. In my books, such a presence means a star. Of course, the young actor was Christopher Plummer. He's a Canadian. I went to school with his father. He's played a hundred and twenty-five parts in rep in Ottawa and Bermuda, of all places."

From youthful ladies' man to young leading man isn't such a mysterious step, but Plummer was promoted in one extraordinary leap. It took him to Paris for the 1955 International Theatre Festival to play Jason—a role first taken by John Gielgud—opposite another First Lady, Judith Anderson, in Robinson Jeffers's *Medea.*

His classical status was established when he returned as Warwick opposite Julie Harris in *The Lark* on

Broadway. And again, summer theatre gave him an important boost. Both Denis Carey as director and Raymond Massey as its first star agreed that Plummer was right for Mark Antony in *Julius Caesar* and Ferdinand in *The Tempest* in 1955 at the new American Shakespeare Festival in Stratford, Connecticut.

What the three Stratford festivals had in common, it seems, is summer, the name of the town, and a vested interest in William Shakespeare's plays. The one in England was housed in a 1920s modish building; in Ontario it was a tent; and in Connecticut, it occupied a theatre that looked Elizabethan outside but was designed to accommodate Broadway touring shows in the winter months. The production's elaborate painted settings did not win admiration as an innovative addition to the field. Yet Plummer came out of it well. Massey wrote: "Roddy McDowell (Ariel), Fritz Weaver (Casca) and, above all, Christopher Plummer's Mark Antony survived." A generous evaluation, since Massey himself played Connecticut's Brutus and Prospero.

Canada's Stratford got the message. After Guthrie left for other projects, his successor Michael Langham invited Plummer to the Festival tent in the summer of 1956. Plummer was to play Henry in Langham's scheme for *Henry V*. Leading Quebecois actors played the French Court: Gratien Gélinas, Jean Gascon, Jean-Louis Roux, Roger Garceau, Guy Hoffmann, Germaine Giroux and Ginette Letondal. Also in the cast were Douglas Campbell, William Hutt, Robert Goodier, Lloyd Bochner, Donald Davis, Robert Christie, Robin Gammell, Max Helpmann, Eric House, David Gardner, Roland Hewgill, Richard Easton, Douglas Rain, Tony Van Bridge, William Needles, Bruno Gerussi, Ted Follows and the revered

Eleanor Stuart (as Queen of France), which makes it about the strongest Stratford ever mustered. Even so, it was Plummer who emerged as the star. "In Mr. Plummer . . . the audience found a crisp, saturnine, magnetic actor. He had the dangerous quality which rivets the attention," I wrote in my record of Stratford from 1953 to 1957.

Stardom was important to Christopher Plummer. That was illustrated when I met the newcomer to Stratford on his arrival. "I wish I were driving up in a red Thunderbird," he declared with an unusual note of nervousness. "You don't need a Thunderbird, Chris," I assured him, "when you have the role of Henry V." He grinned and accepted that consolation.

Langham's casting proved a masterstroke, and Plummer maintained his position against all comers during that glorious season, the last in the old tent. *Henry V*, along with Guthrie's previous *Oedipus Rex,* was invited to the Edinburgh International Festival, giving the British their first glimpse of our brave new classical company—and, incidentally, of its new star. Playing in the Assembly Hall, one inspiration for Tanya Moiseiwitsch's thrust stage, both Canadian productions maintained their original character and won considerable praise. However, the British critics couldn't understand why the French Court spoke broken English. We at home knew, and counted *Henry V* as a true national milestone.

Plummer's Canadian stardom was confirmed when Langham offered him Hamlet to open the new Stratford Festival Theatre in 1957, the pioneer tent turned concrete. This time, Plummer made the concession of also playing Sir Andrew Aguecheek in *Twelfth Night.* Just as well, for his Prince of Denmark followed rather too closely the line of his Henry. But his portrayal of Sir Andrew was responsible for the Festival's loudest laugh; while uttering Sir Andrew's "I was adored once too," his hand slipped and he plunged down the trap door.

Comedy became him the next year—high comedy at that—for he played Benedick opposite Eileen Herlie's Beatrice to great effect. Both of them swore in advance that the other had demanded star billing, so Stratford conceded the double advantage. A glittering pair they were, well matched in star quality. The ladies rather topped him in *The Winter's Tale,* Herlie's Paulina being the showier part and Charmion King's beauteous Hermione commanding the audience's sympathy.

Broadway stardom awaited Plummer the following season in Archibald MacLeish's version of the Book of Job, *J.B.,* again with Massey. This made up for an earlier failed play called *Night of the Auk.* "When do you learn how to choose a play?" he asked me. I could only advise him to depend on trusted counsellors, for some actors never learn that trick. With the classics, the plays are by nature successful. He had no trouble deciding on The Bastard in *King John* and Mercutio in *Romeo and Juliet* back at Stratford. Mercutio was a perfect role for him—all flashing sardonic spirit leading to bitter reproach at the end. But even greater glory lay ahead.

North American admirers of Shakespeare readily acknowledge the superiority of production in England. We tend to attribute greatness in a straight line going right back to Burbage. So the invitation to play leads at Stratford-upon-Avon in 1961 lifted Christopher Plummer to exceptional heights. Moreover, his roles were wonderfully well suited to the Canadian, now a veteran of two other Stratfords. He was to repeat Benedick and to play Richard III. The latter he essayed in the high sardonic vein introduced by John Barrymore and immortalized on stage and film by Sir Laurence Olivier, whom the young Plummer resembled. His demonic glee surpassed the subtler values Alec Guinness had brought to Canada's Stratford in 1953. It is a pity that this new portrayal was never brought to Canada. In addition to the smashing support (Dame Edith Evans was his Margaret in the *Richard*), Plummer was matched opposite Eric Porter in Jean Anouilh's excursion into English history, *Becket*. Plummer scored in the play in London ten months after Laurence Olivier opened it in New York, both playing Henry II. His performance won *The Evening Standard*'s Best Actor of the Year for the Canadian.

Stardom at the original Stratford brought Plummer home to a hero's honours, in this case the indisputably starry roles of Cyrano de Bergerac and Macbeth. His Macbeth, overly dependent on a maternal Lady from Kate Reid, was not a favourite of the critics; but Rostand's gallant with the nose richly made up for that. His was a very sharp, modern interpretation, backed by Langham's sumptuous spectacle, which projected the Canadians into another era of first rate productions.

Broadway also recognized this triple threat Stratford star, and came through with a couple of rewarding roles: Brecht's *Arturo Ui*, which gave him a Hitler clone to match Shakespeare's Richard, and a fierce old Pizarro in another spectacle, *The Royal Hunt of the Sun*. He undertook the younger starring role in the film version; by now films had grown important in the Plummer schedule. *The Sound of Music* opposite Julie Andrews's inspired songbird, won from him a memorable label as "The Sound of Mucus," reflecting the fact that neither of the stars was greatly enriched by the film's phenomenal success, not being on percentage. Along came *Fall of the Roman Empire*, *Inside Daisy Clover*, *The Man Who Would Be King* and, both in 1975, *Return of the Pink Panther* and *Conduct Unbecoming*.

When I congratulated Plummer on returning to Stratford to play in Langham's swan song *Antony and Cleopatra*, he said, "Michael was very naughty to announce it." Plummer's film agent had not cleared it, which meant Langham had to use a stand-by Antony opposite Zoe Caldwell's Cleopatra in rehearsals. When films freed Plummer, it was too late for him to achieve a good relationship with Caldwell. Consequently, Stratford's contribution to international theatre at Montreal's Expo '67 was less than perfect.

Television roles offered quick returns to a man suffering the high costs of being married three times. (The first married him into Broadway society, in the person of Tammy Grimes.) Those TV shots came thick and fast, but he avoided long-term commitments to any series. This allowed him to play Neil Simon's *The Good Doctor*, then to try to revive the Connecticut Stratford by playing a very staccato Iago as counterpoint to the organ tones of James Earl Jones's Othello. Plummer also played his rather bemused Macbeth, this time opposite the executive Glenda Jackson.

Some time later. Plummer succumbed to a largely Canadian-made series, *Counterstrike* (1990). Why? "Because it's the nicest deal. My contract says I only have to work forty-four days a year, so I can do plays and films if I want to. But with the American Stratford gone, the Canadian less classical and the third having found a different kind of Richard, the films will likely have it. I'm getting well paid in my own country, which is particularly fine considering that we all ran away from Canada where there wasn't much to do after you'd done Stratford."

But Chris Plummer was aware of the potential trap of accepting a television series in the middle of one's life. Consequently, he contracted to spend a minimum of his time away from his Connecticut home to film his contribution to TV's *Counterstrike*.

Not long ago he distinguished himself as narrator, with a symphony orchestra playing William Walton's score for Olivier's film of *Henry V*, showing himself eminently able as a live performer. With the London Philharmonic and the Toronto Symphony, he made a sharp distinction between the musical performers and the performer who was his own instrument. On the musical platform, he gave a stunning performance of the actor-as-instrument, every elaborate glance, gesture and stance supplementing his precise control of the high poetic narration with innate musicality

He dispensed with the orchestra when he returned to Stratford on July 13, 1993, to mark the exact anniversary of the Festival. The wayward lad Guthrie once rejected held the stage, solo, in a flattering fund-raiser, for which he contributed his services. He was witty, urbane, glittering with charm, and earned his revenge by making it more a celebration of Plummer than of Guthrie's great contribution to Canadian theatre.

John Colicos

Classical actor born in Toronto in 1928. Educated in Montreal at Commercial High School. First stage work at Canadian Art Theatre, Brae Manor Playhouse, Montreal Repertory Theatre and University Alumnae Dramatic Club in Toronto. Professional debut at Ottawa's Canadian Repertory Theatre, also Bermuda Summer Theatre. London debut in 1953 at Old Vic as Lear. New York debut (1956) in Orson Welles's *King Lear*. Leading roles at American Shakespeare Festival, Stratford Festival, Theatre Toronto. Films include *Anne of a Thousand Days*, *The Postman Always Rings Twice*. Many, many television roles for CBC Drama in Toronto and others including *Galileo*, and *Man and Superman*.

The Shooting Star

Visiting the final resting place of that legendary English actor, Edmund Kean, I was appalled to find church furniture piled on his gravestone. I left a note to complain of this, and, on a whim, signed it "John Colicos." This Canadian actor honours the great tragedian over all other thespians, for he is a Kean-like figure himself. However, his epitaph would have to read "The Shooting Star," rather than Kean's "The Sun's Bright Child."

Of all major Canadian actors and actresses, John Colicos shot up from nowhere to the heights with the greatest speed. That "nowhere" means nowhere theatrically. Born in Toronto, he and his family moved to Montreal where his father was a respected court interpreter. John Colicos decided—after a classroom reading of *Richard II* in which he was given the title role—to concentrate on one language, and with much application he became a master at speaking English.

He had help from Filmore Sadler, teacher of voice at the Montreal Repertory Theatre School, and also from that distinguished coach, Eleanor Stuart. Soon John Colicos was judged acceptable by Rupert Caplan, Montreal producer of CBC English radio drama. He acted juveniles regularly on Caplan's *Way of the Spirit*, the Biblical series Miss Stuart herself played in. Colicos's first stage experiences were less elevated, for he played animals in children's shows for Joy Thomson's Canadian

Art Theatre. But then Sadler invited him to his Brae Manor Summer Theatre, a famous incubator of young Canadian talent.

Colicos was soon playing small but mature roles in *Charley's Aunt* and *The Little Foxes.* He rose to play the John Barrymore role in *The Royal Family of Broadway* and wound up, some seasons later, as Thomas Mendip in *The Lady's Not For Burning*. Having directed him at Brae Manor, I found it easy to cast him in a play at Montreal's Commercial High School when I was invited to direct there. I may even have chosen André Obey's *Noah* with him in mind. (I was complimented for my "lucky and smart casting" in *The Gazette*.) The nineteen year old Colicos was, indeed, very moving as Obey's old patriarch.

I remembered that performance when I moved to *The Globe and Mail.* Astonishingly, Colicos had been accepted by Andrew Allan, CBC's top producer, for his *Stage* series, playing radio dramas along with national voices such as John Drainie, Lorne Greene, Frank Peddie, Jane Mallett and Ruth Springford. When that daring theatrical group, the University Alumnae Drama Club, allowed me to stage Shaw's rare *In Good King Charles's Golden Days* for their entry into the Dominion Drama Festival, Colicos accepted the role of Charles, even though he was wary, as a new professional, of these amateur women. He found himself in good company, as William Needles, Ron Hartmann and Ted Follows were also moonlighting in this DDF production.

The mix of young professionals and serious amateurs proved quite magical as they revealed an unknown Shaw play to the Canadian public. It easily won the Central Ontario Drama Festival and went on to London, Ontario, for the finals of the Dominion Drama Festival. There it was judged by veteran American actor José Ruben. He disliked the play, but did award the Best Actor prize to its King Charles. "What else could he do?" muttered the new professional as he rose to accept the national honour.

Thus encouraged, Colicos decided to try the other London in the early fifties. First he played a season of summer stock in Bermuda, along with other bright Canadians such as Charmion King, Kate Reid and Henry Kaplan. He then approached England, armed with letters from everybody who had any connections there. I gave him one to John Gielgud, which proved useful. Gielgud advised him to join a Shakespearean tour, as walk-on and understudy, and learn the British business that way. This Colicos had the good sense to do, taking off for Helsinki and the Scandinavian countries with an Old Vic tour that starred Stephen Murray in *King Lear*.

The next time Canadians heard of their DDF winner was a picture at the top of *The Globe and Mail*'s front page, announcing that the young Canadian actor had stepped into the role of Lear with the Old Vic in Finland. What's more, John Colicos played the role back at the Old Vic in London. He had, at twenty-three, beaten Edmund Kean's record of playing Richard II at Drury Lane at the early age of twenty-seven.

The year of Colicos's triumph Tyrone Guthrie was casting his first season for Canada's Stratford Festival, and it might have seemed inevitable for him to take advantage of Colicos's phenomenal debut. But Dr. Guthrie was wary of stars, especially cocky young Canadian stars. So Colicos settled for learning the British business in English repertory and the West End. Three years later, he found himself in New York, cast as Edmund in Orson Welles's *King Lear*.

The Colicos penchant for hero-worship was satisfied when he encountered Welles, once a youthful upstart like himself, who had conquered Broadway with his Mercury Theatre and then gone on to sweep Hollywood with *Citizen Kane.* Welles knew that, no matter how great you were on film, it was the stage which proved your true genius, face to face with an audience. When he returned to New York as Lear, Colicos was in his company—the only one who could take over if anything happened to Welles. In time, something did happen to Welles: one broken ankle and another severely sprained. But Colicos discovered that Broadway stars like Welles were tough and competitive: Welles went on as Lear, disguising his wheelchair as a throne. Other actors whom Colicos understudied were to prove more careful—Maurice Evans in *Man and Superman* on television and Alfred Drake as Iago opposite Earl Hyman at Stratford, Connecticut, though Colicos did manage one or two performances there.

Colicos also took over Benedick from Drake when the American Stratford's *Much Ado About Nothing* went on tour. Very good, very dashing he was, too, but he didn't get the notice he might have, what with Kate Hepburn playing Beatrice opposite him. He had to scrounge for strong roles in New York, going off-Broadway to play in *Sergeant Musgrave's Dance.* On Broadway, he played second to Jason Robards in *The Devils.* He rose to *A Man For All Seasons*, but that was in Olney, Maryland; then *Hogan's Goat* and Jean Kerr's *Poor Richard.* He soon settled into the Broadway life, marrying a beautiful model, Mona McHenry, and having two sons—Edmund, named for Edmund Kean, and Nicolas, who followed in his father's footsteps to the London stage. Later Stratford, Connecticut, where he had earlier played Leontes, gave him satisfaction with *Macbeth* in 1967.

When Broadway allowed the leftist Group Theatre to obliterate the sociable New York Theatre Guild, cutting down on the demand for the kind of heroic acting suited to Colicos, Canada still maintained the grand old English traditions at its own Stratford, now under the direction of Michael Langham. Langham sent for Colicos in 1961 to play Aufidius opposite Paul Scofield's Coriolanus as well as Berowne with Zoe Caldwell in *Love's Labour's Lost*, recognizing his true worth. Caliban in the next season's *The Tempest* and Petruchio in *The Taming of the Shrew,* with Kate Reid as his Shrew, were followed by *Troilus and Cressida* and *Cyrano de Bergerac* in 1963, when he took over the role of Cyrano from Christopher Plummer. In the latter part, he was perhaps truer to the high romantic spirit of Rostand's tragic Gascon. John Colicos was a star again, and not without honour in his own country's classical theatre.

"It was a great night for acting last night in Canada. For when John Colicos played Cyrano de Bergerac, the country learned the good news that it had not one but two actors capable of rising to the heights of that great role," started my *Globe and Mail* review from Stratford when the Rostand classic was carried over into the 1963 season with a change of cast. "Mr. Colicos was taking a great gamble, for his predecessor in the role at Stratford, Christopher Plummer, had scored a great personal success.

The first-night audience could not resist making comparisons. But early in the evening, its spontaneous applause showed clearly that Mr. Colicos was being accepted on his own terms and admired strongly. And at the end of the sixth curtain call, the audience's cheering showed that it had experienced a magnificent performance."

John Colicos's first Lear, Old Vic, 1952, *Globe and Mail* front page
photo: Associated Press/Wide World, courtesy *Globe and Mail*

H.W. Whittaker with Christopher Plummer, en route to Edinburgh Festival, 1966

Fred Euringer and Donald Sutherland in *The Tempest* at Hart House, 1957

William Hutt and Kate Reid in *Another Part of the Forest*, DDF, 1949

Then in 1964 came *King Lear*. John Colicos's Lear was not Canada's first glimpse of him in his greatest role. Ironically, in 1953, the year that saw the opening of the tent theatre at Stratford, the year after Colicos played Lear for the Old Vic at home and abroad, the Montreal Festivals invited him to play the role in a vast outdoor production on Mount Royal under Pierre Dagenais's direction—but for one night only.

Colicos's homeland was, unprepared for the theatrical scope and magnificence he unleashed at Stratford. The first review declared his performance to be "of magical power," played "with quite extraordinary beauty, insight and compassion." That opinion in *The Globe and Mail* has been questioned as prejudiced, having been written by myself, yet others were equally enthusiastic. Indeed Robertson Davies, in *The Peterborough Examiner*, accounted Michael Langham's King Lear starring Colicos "the highest achievement of its existence," and this did not exclude the triumphant work of Davies's mentor, Tyrone Guthrie. Even moderates like John Pettigrew declared, "Colicos superb, his final scene truly shattering." Colicos's performance is a milestone in the Stratford Festival's history.

Langham's mastery of the text matched that of his leading player. "Perhaps his finest stroke is that he removes the melodrama from this masterpiece," I observed of the director. He had surrounded the Colicos creation of the old king's "burning through to sanity and truth" with some remarkably worthy performers—Martha Henry as Cordelia, Mervyn Blake the Gloucester, Tony Van Bridge's Kent, Leo Ciceri's Cornwall and Hugh Webster's Fool were splendid realizations. Harking back to that 1964 production, one is inclined to find that Dr. Davies's pronouncement still stands.

Now, while success at Ontario's Stratford has not significantly advanced the careers of most of its actors abroad, Colicos was persuaded to capitalize on his great reviews. Broadway and the West End, film and television, noticed this most talented Canadian, and he did not return to Canada again until 1968. The rocket set off this time had his native strand as launching pad.

Rolf Hochhuth's *The Representative*, examining papal connections with the Nazis, was a sensation in 1964. A couple of years later, the German playwright came out with another accusatory history called *Soldiers*. Laurence Olivier, as head of Britain's National Theatre, was persuaded to produce this controversial work about England's great war hero, Winston Churchill, but the National's board objected strenuously. By an odd quirk of events, two of Canada's pioneer theatres—The Canadian Players and the Crest—collapsed about the same time; and from their ashes rose Theatre Toronto, for which the Welsh director, Clifford Williams, was engaged. He seized the opportunity to give *Soldiers* its English-language premiere. This proved a remarkable success, and much of that was due to Williams's choice of John Colicos to play the Churchill role. In Germany, the central role had been only reminiscent of the great British commander, but Colicos elected to go full-out into impersonation.

His impersonation was uncanny: the famous speech patterns, the bulldog look, the powerful hunch of his shoulders. It brought borrowed force to the bitter play which, even reshaped for the Royal Alexandra stage, was more documentary than drama. The Toronto production, with some changes in cast, was transported to New York (where Roosevelt as war leader had rather overshadowed the British prime minister). Then it was decided to take *Soldiers* over to England to exploit the earlier controversy. The opening was as explosive as anything London had experienced in years. Hochhuth's view of Churchill's conduct of the war during 1943—which resulted in the death of the Polish leader, General Sikorsky—was the bone of much contention. Colicos's impersonation of the British war hero affronted some with its accuracy. "Ubermarionette," spat *The Telegraph*, while *The Times* accounted it "masterly." *The Sunday Express* found no harm done to the memory of the great man and accepted the play as "a magnificent opportunity" for the Canadian actor (as he was identified). Harold Hobson in *The Sunday Times* admitted that Colicos "set one's feelings ablaze" in his scene with Alex Clunes as the Bishop of Chichester, while Philip Hope-Wallace allowed his reservations to diminish in *The Guardian* until he found Colicos's Churchill "quite plausible in the end and out of the Madame Tussaud class."

There were many reservations about Hochhuth's historical drama, both as history and as drama. But on the whole, the British press saluted the Canadian actor as they had few others of that origin. "Masterly" and "magnificent" are not easily come by in London's press, but Colicos won both adjectives—and fairly, too. It was the kind of success that Edmund Kean relished: personal plaudits served on a bed of controversy.

While Colicos had intended to help make Theatre Toronto a significant part of Canadian culture, the success of this one play sent him shooting away from that goal. Film roles followed. Cromwell in *Anne of aThousand Days* opposite Richard Burton's Henry VIII came along in

Britain, and in Hollywood *The Postman Always Rings Twice* with Jack Nicholson and Jessica Lange. It is worth noting that, in both films, Colicos's best work suffered from cutting that centered on the two romantic leads. Yet film and television kept Colicos on America's west coast for some financially profitable years. His return to Canada was marked by an appearance as Sir in *The Dresser* for The Manitoba Theatre Centre, but little stage work seemed to fit in. An invitation to Stratford to play Antony opposite Maggie Smith as Cleopatra had to be refused due to film commitments. Since then, that master of English speech is more often heard serving the anonymity of commercial voice-overs.

Our loss was poignantly resurrected when CBC Stereo broadcast *The Tragedy of King Lear* starring John Colicos in December of 1992, the program emanating from Vancouver studios under the direction of John Juliani. Colicos once again demonstrated his right to the role of the mad old king, giving a most sensitive and powerful interpretation of Shakespeare's text. Lear belongs to Colicos, as he has belonged to few other actors of our century.

William Hutt

Leading Canadian Shakespearean actor. Born in Toronto in 1920. Educated at Vaughan Road Collegiate Institute and Trinity College, University of Toronto. Professional theatre experience began in summer stock at Bracebridge, Ontario. Joined Canadian Repertory Theatre in Ottawa in 1950. Joined first Stratford Festival company in 1953. Toured with Canadian Players from 1954 and on. British debut: *Long Day's Journey Into Night* at Bristol Old Vic. London debut: *Waiting in the Wings*, for Noel Coward. Broadway debut in *Tamburlaine* for Tyrone Guthrie. Played *Tiny Alice* there for John Gielgud. Australian debut: *The Imaginary Invalid* (Stratford Festival tour). Directed *Oscar Remembered* and *Saint Joan* for Stratford Festival. Films: *The Wars* for Robin Phillips, *Models* for Jean-Claude Lord. Television includes role of Sir John A. Macdonald in National Film Board's *The National Dream*. Member of the companies at Shaw Festival and Grand Theatre in London, Ontario.

Our Man of Distinction

William Hutt—star of the Stratford and Shaw festivals, Companion of the Order of Canada, and now a first recipient of the Governor General's Award—is plainly Canadian theatre's "man of distinction." And one of his distinctions is that he achieved that status without ever having to leave home. Not that he hasn't played on stages as far abroad as New York, London and Moscow—and in the best of company. But none of these excursions, I submit, has accounted all that much in winning him his true honours.

And for a country which has long tended to judge its artists by their progress abroad, that is perhaps the greatest distinction of the lot. Another one, equally rare, is that he has a biography on the library shelves, written by fellow-critic Keith Garebian. That gave me pause when I was putting these names together, but then I asked myself if one book was enough to celebrate Sir John Gielgud or Sir Lawrence Olivier?

This piling-up of distinctions in Hutt's own country has allowed Canadians to watch every step of his career, with a few flickering absences spent elsewhere. There's been none of the "what's happening to so-and-so whom we liked so much?" in Bill Hutt's career. This started off, as Garebian reminds us, in a famously conventional fashion: Hutt played the title role in *The Valiant* at his Sunday school. This role is something of a challenge for a teenager, making him an outstanding member of his class.

War intervened soon enough in young Hutt's theatrical beginnings. As Garebian points out, this youngster from Vaughan Road Collegiate "had the height, a big voice, and an ability to transform himself into imaginative settings." Yet it wasn't until he attended Trinity College at the University of Toronto as a young war veteran that the call to use these gifts presented itself.

As a veteran, Hutt had several advantages over other undergraduates in the late forties: confidence, some knowledge of theatre abroad, ambition for a career, and his commanding presence. Perhaps he presumed on them a little too much since Robert Gill, the new director of Hart House Theatre, didn't snap him up for his first production, Shaw's *Saint Joan*.

But in all fairness, he was later given opportunities and availed himself of them with credit. (He was one of the independent undergraduates who crashed the Dominion Drama Festival in 1949 to astonish adjudicator and audience alike with their performances in *Another Part of the Forest*.) Gill knew he was serious, and Gill himself was serious about training talent for the professional theatre, a daring project at that time.

During a summer with the Mark Shawn Players, Hutt snaffled the plum role of Danny in Emlyn Williams's *Night Must Fall*. Then he returned to Hart House Theatre for a second season and was allowed to show his natural bent for comedy in *Jason*, being cast opposite two of Gill's brightest young comediennes, Barbara Hamilton and Anna Cameron. But next time, he was reduced to playing Julius Caesar in Shakespeare's Roman history—an abbreviated and somewhat pompous role.

It was about this time that I first laid eyes on Canada's future Mr. Shakespeare. As new *Globe and Mail* critic, I was much impressed by the professionalism of these undergraduates. My visits to the summer-stock scene and the Canadian Repertory Theatre in Ottawa prepared me for the inclusion of Hutt and some of his fellow undergraduates in the ranks of Stratford that first season.

There was Hutt as Sir Robert Brakenbury, Lieutenant of the Tower of London, and the Duke of Norfolk in the court of Alec Guinness's Richard III. The next season, he graduated to Hortensio, suitor to Barbara Chilcott's Shrew, Froth in *Measure for Measure*, and Leader of the Chorus in *Oedipus Rex*: comedy overshadowing tragedy by two to one. I was to watch his roles get greater and greater over the seasons to come—and more and more serious.

And in between those seasons, the whole country observed his progress as The Canadian Players carried the spirit (if not the pageantry) of Stratford across Canada. Hutt's Warwick had great authority in *Saint Joan* and he won the crown of Prince Hamlet soon after. Lear—the famous Inuit-inspired Lear—was to come in due time.

In Shakespeare's theatre, you had to play the princes and kings to show who is most important—a fact Hutt recognized early on. But it meant he had to sacrifice one of his most instinctive gifts—that for comedy. While on his way up to the heights, Hutt delighted his critics with some witty and hilarious performances. Unforgettable were his paranoiac Ford in *The Merry Wives of Windsor*, his monumentally obsequious Pandarus in *Troilus and Cressida*, and his Khlestakov in *The Government Inspector*.

He climbed new peaks for Jean Gascon in a superb *Tartuffe* and as *The Imaginary Invalid*, which took him to Australia as head of the Stratford company. But my review of his Tartuffe contained the seed of an ongoing concern: "What a wonderful monument to our inherent hypocrisy! Bland, suffering, opportunistic, lecherous and an inspired exploiter of others, this Tartuffe repels us as much as—or more than—he convulses us." Was Hutt encouraged by his director to stress the sinister anticlerical aspect?

(When I complimented Robert Prevost on his superb design for this production, I mentioned the luminous cross in the ceiling which introduced Gascon's production. Prevost took no credit for that, saying it came out of Gascon's Quebecois background.)

True, the path of history is paved with the fall of monarchs rather than the pratfalls of clowns. Hutt, biding his time as others came to the lists, established his right to play Prospero, Richard II, King Lear, Titus Andronicus, the Duke in *Measure*, as well as such grave gems as Uncle Vanya, James Tyrone in *Long Day's Journey into Night*, and Anton Schill, the mayor in *The Visit*.

Yet all his prowess was not solemn and kingly. He made history as Lady Bracknell for Robin Phillips by finding his own way to say "a handbag!" And he ventured into drag again for *Arsenic and Old Lace*. But that was in London's Grand Theatre and was balanced by a *Timon of Athens* in Robin Phillips's venturesome season there.

Certainly, Hutt worked well with Phillips. Vancouver called the actor to play Sir Thomas More in *A Man for All Seasons*, and then the Shaw Festival reached out for him to expound a number of Shavian leads, all well within his provenance.

My favourite there was his Sir William Gower in Pinero's *Trelawney of the Wells*, for he played the old man who remembered Kean with a delightful sense of the ridiculous underlying the pathos, glossed only lightly by pomposity. "A gift unused can be lost, but Hutt shows that his comic spirit has not been entirely subdued by the years of solemnity."

To my surprise, my appreciation of his performance brought forward a response characteristic of the proudest of actors: "For years, I have laboured under the assumption that it is 'unprofessional' to thank a critic for his approving reviews," he wrote. "Crowding seventy as I am, I am going to throw caution and/or protocol to the winds and thank you for your years of encouragement, support and expert guidance...."

Hutt went on to speak as the proud but worried actor: "Is there a real reconciliation between Gower and grandson? Does Gower really accept that grandson as a 'gypsy?' Do grandson and Rose really get together? Perhaps Pinero didn't want to answer the questions, leaving the audiences in a state of misty-eyed suspense." (Signed) Bill.

It pleased a lot of faithful Stratford-goers when David William invited Hutt back for his 1993 season, the last for this artistic director, to repeat his role of *The Imaginary Invalid*.

Before that happened, William Hutt received the call to Ottawa as one of the first recipients of those new Governor General's Awards, a startling counterpoint to what the artistic community believed was the government's neglect of the arts. Others of theatrical distinction were to be honoured: Gweneth Lloyd, founder of the Royal Winnipeg Ballet, Oscar Peterson and Norman Jewison, with Donald Sutherland, Monique Mercure and Celia Franca as presenters. But Hutt managed one more rare distinction among them. He was too busy working at London's Grand Theatre to attend the award ceremonies at the National Arts Centre in January 1993.

So television and film, an actor's friends in this wide country, brought Hutt's grateful thanks to Ottawa and national audiences. He was introduced by Richard Monette, who was making his first public appearance as the Stratford Festival's artistic director elect. Monette, too, spoke of "this bright particular star" not only for his success in measuring himself in the great roles but also for his ability to play the clowns. Television then reminded us that it had not overlooked his talent by showing video clips from his many impersonations for the medium, including those of George Bernard Shaw and John A. Macdonald. Then videotape brought us William Ian DeWitt Hutt in person, bedecked with his new honour by the First Lady of the Grand Theatre, Martha Henry. Juggling the two audiences—one in London, Ontario, the other in Ottawa—Hutt spoke of the tussle between viceregal honours and the demands of a theatrical career. But he managed to avoid consoling the other recipients for being "at liberty" and was delighted to be one of them in receipt of this “singularly prestigious accolade.”

Another distinction chalked up, with the warm feeling that he would be back where he belonged—at centre stage at the Stratford Festival. Another proud veteran was welcomed home to play classical comedy by Molière: a comedian of high distinction once again.

Kate Reid

Actress, born in England in 1930. Educated at Havergal College in Toronto and at The Royal Conservatory of Music, University of Toronto. Began stage career at Hart House Theatre, University of Toronto. Early professional roles with Straw Hat Players and Crest Theatre. Starred in *The Three Sisters*, *Gaslight*, *The Rainmaker*, *The Stepmother* (in West End, London). Played Stratford Festival in *The Cherry Orchard*, *The Taming of the Shrew*, *Macbeth*, among others. In New York: *Who's Afraid of Virginia Woolf?*, *Dylan*, *Slapstick Tragedy*, later *The Price*, *Death of a Salesman*, and others. Shaw Festival and other regional theatres. Films: *The Andromeda Strain*, *A Delicate Balance*. Radio: *White Oaks of Jalna, Disraeli*. Died 1993.

Why, There's a Wench!

Before Stratford existed, the finals of the Dominion Drama Festival were the great national event of the theatrical year. In the thirties and forties, the winners of the country's regional competitions vied for pride of place as well as prestigious awards. By 1949, the DDF Finals were important enough to rate the country's prime touring house, the Royal Alexandra Theatre in Toronto.

That year, the winner was *Another Part of the Forest,* Lillian Hellman's sequel to *The Little Foxes,* staged by an independent group of Robert Gill's students at the University of Toronto's Hart House. If any of the actors, directors, governors or committee members involved could have seen into the future, they might have spotted this as the beginning of the end for the DDF, for it was by nature encouraging the more polished theatre that was to replace it. A significant step towards professionalism was being taken here.

Anna Cameron had organized fellow students sharing Gill's training at Hart House Theatre, a purely voluntary program. From their ranks, she and student director Henry Kaplan picked such budding talents as William Hutt, Eric House, Ted Follows, "and a big-eyed little girl from the Royal Conservatory classes," Kate Reid. Together, they walked off with the Festival's top honours. As new critic of *The Globe and Mail* that year, I was astonished that university students could be so professional and so good in such serious drama as this. The adjudicator, Philip

Hope-Wallace, a fellow critic and good friend of the Festival, was equally astonished.

Later, when Robert Gill staged Terence Rattigan's dramatization of *Crime and Punishment* at Hart House, I was again struck by the luminous quality of young Miss Reid's acting. It equalled for me Lillian Gish's haunting performance in the Broadway production that had been staged by Fyodor Komisarjevsky for John Gielgud. Here was a young talent of rare emotional beauty.

These Gill actors, schooled in professionalism by this earnest director from Carnegie Tech, took their first professional flights in summer. Three Gill alumni, Murray and Donald Davis along with Charmion King, assisted by some preparatory work by Gill, launched The Straw Hat Players in their cottage country of Muskoka. There I caught up with them in my efforts to keep my *Globe and Mail* column space dedicated to theatre.

Kate Reid was the baby of the Straw Hatters. She was a particular favourite of James Hozack, the popular Hart House manager who also took on this summer venture. Once, while I was having a drink with him after a show one night, chatting about the actors under his care, he suddenly dropped his voice to mention Katie Reid, aware that she was eavesdropping. Despite his precaution, the mention of her name brought a sudden pounding from her on the wall that divided us.

When winter took these aspiring actresses to New York, I was invited to visit Anna Cameron, Barbara Hamilton and Kate in their shared apartment. I did so, and came upon Kate with her head in the fireplace, a tumbler to her ear. She was eavesdropping again, this time on the mother of the Gabor sisters, who was entertaining a gentleman next door. If the ability to listen is a prime requisite for a good actor, then Kate Reid acquired it early on. She also learned to listen to directors; that is to some degree a key to her theatrical success.

There were other summer theatres in Kate Reid's preparations for professionalism. At the Peterborough Summer Theatre, she acquired valuable experience, a husband in Michael Sadlier (the theatre's producer), and a leading role in Robertson Davies's important new play, *At My Heart's Core,* written with her in mind. That was in 1950. In Bermuda, she was part of the all-Canadian company that played in the Bermudiana Hotel. At Vineland, Ontario, she played in *The Rainmaker*, which almost took her to London's West End. (Unfortunately, her mother's illness forced her to come home, and Geraldine Page replaced her.)

Kate Reid didn't have to go abroad to acquire an extraordinary series of opportunities in the theatre. Here in Canada, a variety of important roles developed her special style and range. The Crest Theatre, founded in 1954 by the Davis brothers from Muskoka, cast her as Nina in Jack Landau's fine production of *The Three Sisters,* with Charmion King and Amelia Hall as the other Chekhov siblings. "Miss Reid's sense of frustration is beautifully balanced by the gaiety she can achieve; . . . a fine distinctive actress at her very best," my *Globe* review decided. ("An artistic accomplishment by any test," admitted Nathan Cohen in *The Toronto Star*.)

Within the same 1955 season, she scored equally well in *The Rainmaker*, which moved later to Vineland. She also repeated her former DDF role as Birdie in *The Little Foxes* and played the lead in *Gaslight.* But she was not limited to her own home town over the next few years. She played Mavor Moore's *The Ottawa* Man for the

Charlottetown Festival, *The Subject Was Roses* in Ottawa, and *Leaving Home* in Vancouver, starring with Leslie Yeo. The David French drama had started out in Toronto's small Tarragon Theatre but became a full-scale star vehicle when it reached the Playhouse.

Not only was this *Leaving Home* larger in scale, but it was also expanded in content; and Kate Reid helped make it so. As my *Globe* review of November 15, 1973, pointed out, "The Playhouse has imported one of the country's leading actresses to play the mother, thus giving the conflict further dimension. With Kate Reid fighting Mrs. Mercer's quiet battle for the love of her sons, the father's role is seen in a different perspective. French's autobiographical drama acquires a new maturity.

"Miss Reid makes Mary Mercer an opponent of equal weight in the ring. She marshals the family forces with the confidence of an old campaigner, building the father's position as the irrational despot. The love she communicates for the two sons is made very apparent by her strong emotional playing, but she makes it perfectly clear where her true love and loyalty must lie. The scene in which she closes the play and explains why she married Jacob Mercer is beautifully handled."

My review continued: "Vancouver is seeing the talented Miss Reid both on stage and in good company on film. *A Delicate Balance* [is playing] at four local theatres with the Canadian actress keeping well up with her fellow players, Katherine Hepburn and Paul Scofield." It's worth noting that the former ingenue of the Straw Hat Players was by now the mother of two children, Reid and Robin, by Austin Willis, after divorcing Michael Sadlier.

However, it was the Stratford Festival which gave Kate Reid her true star status. No other Canadian actress, I venture to say, ever had such opportunity, although Frances Hyland, Martha Henry and Lucy Peacock would be hard on her heels. In fact, Regina's Hyland had already scaled the West End heights when Guthrie brought her back to Canada, which she had left as a student. Henry and Peacock both progressed through the National Theatre School, although the former had first made her name as Martha Buhs at the Crest Theatre.

Michael Langham especially appreciated the unusual range of Kate Reid. Although she looked like an ingenue, she was capable of an emotional power beyond her years. Langham explored that versatility, casting her first as Celia in *As You Like It*—the most ingenue of roles—and as the outspoken Emilia in *Othello* opposite Douglas Rain, whose Iago seemed quite definitive. That "double" paid off for Langham, and he continued to give his discovery contrasting roles. What greater opposites than the randy old Nurse in *Romeo and Juliet* and the abandoned Helena in *A Midsummer Night's Dream*? Well, you might name the noble victim of royal passion—Katharine of Aragon in *Henry VIII*—along with Jacquenetta, the wench who captivates Don Amadeo in *Love's Labour's Lost,* which followed. With the distinguished Paul Scofield as her Amadeo, they provided one of the reasons that this Langham production became a Stratford legend.

That was in 1962, a beacon year for Kate Reid, for she also played her first major role on Broadway—Martha, in Edward Albee's sensational *Who's Afraid of Virginia Woolf?*—if only on matinees. Walking across Times Square with her after an overpowering performance, I relished her confession that she had to believe in Martha's non-existent son to be able to cope with the tremendous emotional demands that Albee's heroine made on her. She shivered as we walked and talked in the rain.

Happily, that excursion into what Canadians thought of as "the big time" did not break her triumphant progress at Stratford. She was the very physical Lady Macbeth opposite Christopher Plummer's Oedipal thane in a controversial *Macbeth,* during the same season that she matched John Colicos's flamboyant Petruchio as Katharine in *The Taming of the Shrew.* In another of Langham's most admired productions, *Troilus and Cressida,* she was the wild prophetess Cassandra as well as playing the exasperated Adriana in *The Comedy of Errors. By* 1965, she was the more patient Portia in *Julius Caesar*, and the restless Madame Raneveskaya in John Hirsch's fervent staging of *The Cherry Orchard.* This latter performance in a major part led an early Stratford graduate, Timothy Findley, to proclaim that she had given "her most accomplished interpretation of a classic role." That Chekhov performance may be said to have climaxed her Stratford years. Never before had any member of its company been given such opportunities or fulfilled them so well—with such emotion, intensity, vulnerability and mischievous fun.

New York could not be resisted any longer. Stratford was, after all, a summer paradise; but she had to face the cold competition of a metropolitan winter. Her matinees as Martha had been noticed. Playwrights in particular had paid attention, among them such pre-eminent ones as Arthur Miller and Tennessee Williams, rivals for the American crown relinquished by Eugene O'Neill.

First came an opportunity to match her strength against another world-famous actor, Alec Guinness. Although he had not admired Dylan Thomas when they met, Guinness recognized the dramatic value Sidney

Michael invested in him with *Dylan*.

The rich role of Dylan's wife Caitlin was a prize for the actress exploring a New York career. And her home town of Toronto got to appreciate her in it first, for it premiered there at the O'Keefe Centre. Competing with O'Keefe's size and a star who refused to "impersonate" Dylan was enough to make anybody insecure, but Kate Reid managed to invest that quality into her playing of the neurotic woman who loved the hard-drinking poet. Guinness declared her performance "divine." She was proving herself ready for "the big time."

New York agreed, giving the young Canadian her first Tony Award nomination. Another came for her work in *Slapstick Tragedy,* where she withstood comparison with two other talented imports, England's Margaret Leighton and Australia's Zoe Caldwell. Her Stratford admirer, Tiff Findley, declared that Tennessee Williams wrote this play with her in mind. He made the same claim for her with Arthur Miller's *The Price.* If so, this gives Kate Reid rare distinction in American theatre. Miller not only wrote *The Price* but also took over its direction in Robert Whitehead's production. That was in the 1970 Broadway season and *The Price* took her to London after that New York premiere. Fifteen years later, she portrayed Linda Loman in a much-publicized, filmed and revived *Death of a Salesman*, playing opposite Dustin Hoffman as Willie. This was world theatre with a world cinema cachet.

Between these two Miller works, there were other Broadway shows of note. She played Big Mama in a successful revival of Williams's *Cat on a Hot Tin Roof,* was in Brian Friel's *Freedom of the City,* and scored in John Guare's *Bosoms and Neglect.* Now, invitations came from across the United States for her. She played New Haven's

Long Wharf Theatre, Philadelphia's Chestnut Street Theatre, and the Connecticut Stratford's American Shakespeare Festival, repeating her Nurse in *Romeo and Juliet* as well as playing Gertrude in *Hamlet*. Then she came back to Canada to play Clytemnestra for John Woods at the National Arts Centre in Ottawa, and settled down in Niagara-on-theLake for the Shaw Festival.

It was in that festival's revival of Somerset Maugham's *The Circle* that I observed a curious phenomenon. Mature enough to play its disgraced, bedizened Lady Kitty (with appropriate make-up and costume), her bright spirit instead gave the lie to all this and to Lady Kitty as a warning to the next generation. Lady Kitty shone forth like the bright star Kate Reid undoubtedly was.

But even the most glowingly youthful of actresses can suffer physical disability and fragility. When next I saw Kate, she was a sad victim of arthritis. It was in a revival of *Arsenic and Old Lace*, reuniting her at Hart House with Charmion King and "Hank" Kaplan as director. It was not a happy reunion. For one thing the stairs betrayed the actress, and, even with extra handrails, she could not conceal her difficulty in using them.

Her painful disability was also evident in Stratford's 1992 *Uncle Vanya*, staged at the newly named Tom Patterson Theatre. Cast as the old nurse Marina, she was placed at one end of the long open stage and had to struggle to join the play's action. But on that same stage, the next night, there she was as one of the two guardian aunts in her second Michel Tremblay revival for Stratford, *Bonjour, la, bonjour*, playing in support of her old friend, Douglas Rain, the actor's actor. That night Kate was herself again, in service to a Canadian playwright of importance, just as she had served Tennessee Williams, Arthur Miller and Edward Albee down south, and earlier Robertson Davies and David French in Canada. Just as she had illuminated the inherited glories of Chekhov, Shaw and Shakespeare for us.

It was appropriate that Stratford's fortieth season gave her yet another contrasting role, as Mistress Overdone in *Measure for Measure*, working under Michael Langham's direction. Kate Reid was home again.

And at home she died, quite suddenly, on March 27, 1993, after being brought back from filming in Texas. The diagnosis: brain tumors. A luminous talent dimmed at only sixty-two years, but with a great contribution to our theatre to her credit. She was much mourned. John Colicos, her 1962 Petruchio, spoke of the high emotional element in her acting and the consequences for her off-stage existence. Colicos, and most of her obituary notices, measured her achievement by her work abroad. Ironically, my *Oxford Companion to American Theatre* does not mention either Kate Reid or John Colicos. But the *Oxford Companion to Canadian Theatre* features them both, with biographies and pictures, as important contributors to our growing theatre. Old colonial habits die hard; we measure ourselves by a long ago Broadway—or Hollywood.

Donald Sutherland

Born in Saint John, New Brunswick, in 1934. Educated in Nova Scotia and at the University of Toronto. Theatrical debut there at Hart House Theatre in *The Male Animal.* Studied at London Academy of Drama and Music (1957). London debut in *August for the People* (1961). Films since 1964 have included *Castle of the Living Dead*, *M*A*S*H*, *Klute*, *Ordinary People*, *Casanova*. Television since 1963 includes *Oedipus Rex*, *Hamlet at Elsinore*, *The Avengers*, *Bethune*. Broadway debut in *Lolita* (1981).

The Ungainly Star

The sad story of Donald Sutherland is the shortest and the least theatrical of these personal memories. You might say I include it only to quote from *Playboy*, a magazine rarely thought of by theatre researchers. Yet Don Sutherland is another of the Canadians who soared to stardom, and so is a genuine "name-drop."

Like Plummer and Colicos, Sutherland emerged among his school mates as an eccentric. Like them he was touched by Dionysus, had the gift of Thespis, and the Protean touch. Like them, he responded to the siren call of the electronic performance. Of the three actors, he succumbed to mass media earliest and most successfully. As you can see, it is hard to feel sorry for him, to see his as a wasted life—save by some tenacious old drama critic fond of his theatrical discoveries.

With Sutherland's career in theatre so short, I have space to try to recreate the kind of student production which centered around Hart House at the University of Toronto in those great days of Robert Gill. That gifted professional strove to release the latent acting talents he encountered there into an uncaring world; and he did so with remarkable success.

I say "around Hart House," but should say literally beneath it, for Hart House Theatre was, both physically and symbolically, in the basement of this student union building. (Not far from it and just up Queen's Park Crescent, the New Play Society, Jupiter Theatre and

Young People's Theatre all started up in another basement—that of the Royal Ontario Museum.) Vincent Massey had the inspiration of replacing a Hart House shooting gallery with this underground theatre, being himself a gentleman player of talent.

I first explored this cavern of delight in 1949, courtesy of an invitation from the Trinity College Dramatic Society to direct its student production, a dramatization of *Vanity Fair*. Other student engagements followed, as well as productions staged at Hart House for the Central Ontario Drama Festival, then in full flourish. In the course of such involvements, I made friends with the theatre's manager, the very humourous James Hozack, with the production assistant, Marian Walker, and with the great man himself, Bob Gill.

It came my turn to direct Victoria College's student drama. This meant I could pick the play, cast it, design and direct it, using Victoria College students as actors. Fascinated by Jean Giraudoux at the time, having done *The Enchanted* for Trinity College, I picked his adaptation of Sophocles' *Electra*, despite its great length. I detailed a clever student, Terry Shiels, to make a cut version. We avoided the Greek-laundry look by costuming it in the decade in which it was written, the 1930s, which still made it seem like historical garb for the young cast. Its setting of Agamemnon's Palace gave me an opportunity to recreate the theatre's own proscenium on its stage, with a branch added to suggest a park, a stairway for the palace. For furniture, I borrowed a garden table-cum-bench from my neighbours on Prince Arthur. The whole effect was meant to be classical French rather than classical Greek.

Casting involved picking nine young girls to make up the chorus, dressed in traditional *lycée* uniforms. That was easy—height counted. For Electra, Jane Griffen (later Curnwath) had just the right quality; but for Clytemnestra, I believe we had to go outside the college when we cast Arlene Kamens. Fred Euringer, John Douglas, Bob Remnant and Terry Shiels himself were also good choices. Then we came to Orestes. What we did not need in this sophisticated French view of a Greek classic was somebody too tall, terribly awkward, and with a strong Maritimes accent. Don Sutherland was all of those things—the adjectives were later applied to him in London by West End critics.

But I had seen this kid from New Brunswick in his debut for Bob Gill as Wally, the football player, in *The Male Animal*, and I recognized the spark. So did the whole audience, by its laughter. Sure, he was gangly and clumsy and too tall, especially in an ice cream suit of the thirties. To minimize his height, I had him enter and sit down before the women came on for their scenes. Real life to the contrary, some balance of height is decreed on stage. But sitting or standing, Donald Sutherland compelled attention and commanded believability.

That was in 1956. Next season, Bob Gill was staging *The Tempest*. Remembering Wally, he cast the Maritime kid in the comic role of Stephano. By that time, young Sutherland had done some summer stock and was definitely interested in theatre. Seriously. So he gambled, all or nothing. He has told the story many times since—on the air, in public, and to me. I'll use the version he related to Claudia Dreyfus of *Playboy* magazine: "When I was a boy, I never wanted to be a movie actor. The idea of being a stage actor was fine. Hollywood was . . . never-never land; real people didn't live there. No one from Nova Scotia ever got there. I decided to study drama at the

University of Toronto. Towards the end, I had this small part in *The Tempest*—a hard part. I prepared very carefully.

"There was this very influential critic at *The Globe and Mail*, Herbert Whittaker. So I said to myself, if he likes what I've done, I'll become an actor. If he doesn't, I'll quit." (The *Playboy* interviewer prompted him: "And?") "And he wrote, 'Donald Sutherland has a spark of talent which illumes the stage.' So the year after my graduation, when I was twenty-three, I went to England to study at the London Academy of Music and Dramatic Art."

He was completely miserable there. He swore his voice teacher, the celebrated Iris Warren, "hated my guts." He broke away, got married, did repertory for a year in Scotland and then around England. At one point, he met up with two other refugees from Hart House, Jackie Burroughs and Bill Davis. Together, they staged the two-hander, *Two for the Seesaw,* Davis directing. When I encountered him next—he took me to a rock concert at London's Festival Hall—he had already done his first "spaghetti western," *Castle of the Living Dead,* made in Italy. I should have warned him then, but didn't. One film led to another and soon it was too late: we'd lost one of our most instinctive stage actors. Films suited Don Sutherland and he suited films. (Nobody is ever too tall or too short on screen.) He wangled his way into Chris Plummer's *Oedipus the King,* playing Leader of the Chorus. (When I saw this film, I thought that Iris Warren hadn't done a bad job for him. Then I realized that his voice, along with those of the Greek actors, had been dubbed!)

He got into *The Dirty Dozen* when Clint Eastwood proved difficult. He got into *Klute* (which got him Jane

Fonda, on and off) and *M*A*S*H,* which got him a very big public. He got Fellini's *Casanova*, which got him into the ranks of producer. That added film producer to his list of occupations—along with radio announcer, disc jockey, mine worker (in Finland, no less) and London actor. He had made his debut there at the Royal Court Theatre in *August for the People,* also playing *Spoon River Anthology*. But it was a long, long time before the list included Broadway star.

That came late in 1981 at the Brooks Atkinson Theatre when he starred in Edward Albee's dramatization of Vladimir Nabokov's *Lolita*. It was a stormy time for him and for everybody else, for by then he was in the habit of fighting to get what he wanted in films. Besides, the producer ran out of money, which gave playwright Albee the upper hand. The only ally Sutherland had was the British actor, Ian Richardson. The critics were not kind, perhaps resenting a film star thinking he could dazzle Broadway in a role as unappealing as Humbert Humbert.

Yet the truth is that Donald Sutherland had lost none of his gift—his ability to command the stage. The spark which illumined the Hart House stage in *The Tempest* so long ago had burst forth to brighten Broadway. Stardom in films, the money and the life it offered suited him splendidly—better than the formal patterns of the theatre would. But I still can't help wishing that he would accept another invitation to perform at Stratford. Perhaps one has to wait longer for his *King Lear*. Then one recalls that Raymond Massey, another Canadian who turned to filmdom, waited all his life to return to the stage as Lear, only to find that his legs had given out before he did.

John Gielgud

Actor/director, born in London in 1904. Educated at Westminster School, Lady Benson's School, and Royal Academy of Dramatic Art. Debut at the Old Vic Theatre in *Henry V*, 1921; later at Oxford Playhouse. Succeeded Noel Coward in *The Vortex* and *Constant Nymph*. Trophimov in *The Cherry Orchard,* Lyric Theatre, Hammersmith. Joined Old Vic in 1929; principal roles of Romeo, Mark Antony, Macbeth, Hamlet. In West End: Richard of Bordeaux, Hamlet, Richard II, Joseph Surface, Vershinin in *The Three Sisters*, Shylock, John Worthing. Toured for ENSA troop shows. In New York: *Crime and Punishment*, *The Importance of Being Earnest*, *Love for Love*, also on tour. Outstanding roles since: Thomas Mendip in *The Lady's Not for Burning:* Angelo, Leontes, Ivanov, Benedick, Lear. Modern roles in *Bingo*, *Home*, *No Man's Land*. Directed *The Chalk Garden*, *The Trojans* at Covent Garden; also *The Complaisant Lover*, *Five Finger Exercise*. Toured solo in *The Ages of Man*. Author of several books, starting with *Early Stages* in 1939. Many film appearances. Knighted in 1953; Companion of Honour in 1988.

Richard Burton

Actor born in 1925 in Pontrhydfed, Wales, educated at Exeter College, Oxford. Debut at Royal Court, Liverpool, in *Druid's Rest*. R.A.F. 1944-47. In West End: *The Lady's Not for Burning* in 1949, also in New York. *Hamlet* at the Old Vic in 1953, also Sir Toby Belch, Caliban, Othello. *Hamlet* at Edinburgh Festival, repeated in Toronto and New York, 1964. In New York: *Legend of Lovers*, *Time Remembered.* Toronto and New York: Arthur in *Camelot,* 1960. Films include *My Cousin Rachel, The Robe, Becket, Who's Afraid of Virginia Woolf?*, *Dr. Faustus*. Died in 1984.

A Tale of Two Hamlets

A small group of hangers-on at the Montreal Repertory Theatre was planning to take a train to Toronto to see the century's greatest Hamlet. But then the exciting news came that John Gielgud's greatest success in England would also come to His Majesty's Theatre before opening on Broadway. By then, we knew that Guthrie McClintic was directing, Jo Mielziner designing; Judith Anderson was the Gertrude and Lillian Gish the Ophelia. Such plums were rare in 1936, especially in Montreal, which hadn't maintained its place on the American touring circuit.

However, our high hopes were dashed after all. His Majesty's was owned by Consolidated Theatres, which also owned the bigger film houses in town. Consolidated preferred its entertainment delivered in cans, not arriving by train. No bags, baskets or union rules, or temperamental actors who had to be coddled and promoted before the box office worked. So Consolidated let us down again, too late for us to make that trip to Toronto.

Instead, we read about the Hamlet that got away in *The New York Times*, in *Stage Magazine* and in *Theatre Arts,* whose editor Rosamund Gilder devoted a whole book to the Gielgud Hamlet. We also heard about the Toronto production, which opened after two days of frantic dress rehearsals in its sumptuous Van Dyck staging. Gielgud, whose fourth Hamlet it was, had insisted on changes in McClintic's direction at the last moment.

Had we read *The Globe* (yet to don its *Mail*), we might have been consoled. True, Dr. Laurence Mason's review was headed "A Glorious Hamlet." But that seemed to refer to the McClintic production: "This is first-class, up-to-date stagecraft, worthy of the matchless material dealt with."

Of the acting, Dr. Mason had some doubts. "John Gielgud is undoubtedly a fine Hamlet, though discussion is possible as to whether he has the weight, power and magnetic personality enough to be a great one!" This sounds like treason, as does the critic's complaint that Judith Anderson is almost negative as the Queen, and Lillian Gish is "not an electrifying Ophelia."

Then comes something like an explanation. Dr. Mason claimed that "for a first night performance, this was remarkably smooth and finished. If some of the suggestions above are adopted, it will run even better." His "suggestions" dealt with audibility and pace. Not even the amplified Ghost escaped his charge of inaudibility. My distinguished predecessor was well aware of what happened to actors when suddenly engulfed by costume, scenery and light changes. Dress rehearsals belong to the designers, never to actors.

This terrible fact must have stayed in John Gielgud's mind. Toronto problems ironed out, this *Hamlet* went on to become the toast of New York, with ovations and cheering on the second night as well as on the first. The production even broke John Barrymore's old record of one hundred and one performances of *Hamlet*.

I never caught up with that *Hamlet*, which I still regret more than fifty years later. But I saw enough of Gielgud's work to agree that he was the outstanding classical actor of his century. He was also an extremely versatile actor,

John Gielgud, 1937 Hamlet

Richard Burton,
rehearsing for *Hamlet*, 1964

THEATRICAL HELPERS

Michel Saint-Denis, cartoon by "Papas," c. 1950

Tyrone Guthrie in rehearsal, 1959

Brecht collage of Charles Laughton, 1945

playing the work of many playwrights as superbly as he played Shakespeare's.

I first saw him portraying a burly old peasant in André Obey's *Noah,* and next, in utter contrast, as John Worthing in a perfect production of *The Importance of Being Earnest.* He was the epitome of Restoration Comedy in *Love for Love,* of Old Comedy in *The School for Scandal,* compelling as the deathseeking hero of *The Lady's Not for Burning* and as the importunate poet in *No Man's Land.* Certainly, I will never match in my lifetime Gielgud's Benedick opposite Peggy Ashcroft in *Much Ado About Nothing,* or his pathologically jealous Leontes of *A Winter's Tale.* His Lear survived the extraordinary designs created for the production by Noguchi; and his Prospero, which was directed by a youthful Peter Brook, was another definitive creation.

But sad to say, I never saw his Hamlet.

Years later on a working holiday in London (I rarely took any other kind), I was commissioned by the Canadian Broadcasting Corporation to interview John Gielgud about playing Shakespeare's greatest role. Arriving at his small house in Westminster, I was joined by a technician from the British Broadcasting Corporation who was to do the recording for me. The doorbell gave no response. We rang again. No luck. We were preparing to depart when a very small car drew up and the tall slender figure of Sir John emerged. "Why, Herbert Whittaker," he said, "what are you doing here?" (We had met when *The Importance* came to Montreal and the Montreal Repertory Theatre feted him.) I explained. True, he replied, the CBC had invited him to do the interview with me, but no date had been set. However, he graciously invited us to come in anyway, and we would see what we could do.

What he could do was quite extraordinary. Nobody ever talked so well on any theatre subject as Gielgud, and on Hamlet he was astonishing. My contribution was the occasional "oh?" or "you mean . . ?" The flow of his remembrances came without notes or looking up references for dates—unbroken until the BBC man ran out of the huge disks on which he was recording this flow of brilliance.

That was the closest I ever got to the Gielgud *Hamlet*. But it was enough to give me a whole new vision of the play and where its greatness lay.

In 1958, Sir John visited Stratford's Festival Theatre to introduce North Americans to his legendary recital of Shakespeare, *The Ages of Man*. On that occasion, he gave us an excerpt from *Hamlet*, along with all the great roles he had played and many lesser ones he had not. That compensated me somewhat, the sight of Sir John taking the measure of our celebrated stage and making extraordinary use of it.

Although not an ideal home for legitimate drama, Toronto's O'Keefe Centre regularly welcomed actors and actresses of high repute. In the winter of 1964, the announcement came that Richard Burton would rehearse and perform his Hamlet there prior to Broadway—and under the direction of Sir John Gielgud.

O'Keefe had welcomed Sir Laurence Olivier in *Becket* in 1961, playing the King superbly on opening night, though less so later in the week. (When I discovered this, I complained to another theatrical knight, Sir Cedric Hardwicke, about actors not living up to their opening nights. "You don't ask an opera star to sing *Tosca* eight nights a week," came the answer from that wise old bird who was performing at the Royal Alex during the same period. "What's the answer?" I demanded. "Repertory," said Sir Cedric, looking even wiser.)

Britain's other members of the reigning theatrical triumvirate, Sir Ralph Richardson and Gielgud, played at O'Keefe in *The School for Scandal* the following year. Sir John complained about the barn-like size of the house. So did Sir Ralph, who refused to return there when next asked. Yet Alec Guinness played *Dylan* at O'Keefe opposite Kate Reid the same year. But Gielgud's latest production of *Hamlet* was different. This was Shakespeare where speech was all.

This *Hamlet* turned out to be different, all right. For one thing, Elizabeth Taylor accompanied her great love, Richard Burton, and the unholy union of these two stars affected staid Toronto in the most extraordinary ways. From the moment their plane landed, the two darlings of the public were hounded, screamed at and ogled everywhere they went. Elizabeth Taylor could not even walk her dogs. The police had the couple under guard twenty-four hours a day, with their vice-regal suite at the King Edward Hotel as the focus of the heaviest security. Eileen Herlie, who was to play Gertrude (she had also been Olivier's Gertrude in his film), said she felt as if she were in prison.

The pressure of this public scrutiny started to tell on the production's rehearsals. "Oh, I wish Elizabeth would take the children and go away somewhere!" cried Sir John. Hume Cronyn demurred: "No, no. Elizabeth is the professional one, always on stage on time. Although she can drink him under the table, she makes sure he turns up when rehearsal is called." Cronyn had spent a year with the couple in Rome when they were filming *Cleopatra*.

I met the lady only once—when I was interviewing

Burton at an O'Keefe gathering. She opened her great violet eyes, with their incredible double eyelashes, and said "I'm sick." He paid no heed, so she wandered off—to be sick, I suppose.

During the interview, Burton remarked that he would stop drinking while he was rehearsing *Hamlet. The Globe* excerpted this proclamation from my interview and put it on the front page, which shows the madness of the day. Gullible *Globe*!

The production was reported extensively in a book by its Guildenstern, William Redfield. Since he felt unhappy and neglected, he described an unhappy company. When Toronto critics found the opening night unsatisfactory, Redfield was unhappy about that too. The Canadian member of the cast, Hume Cronyn, came out of it best, playing Polonius. Cronyn was "no fool but a wise man capable of stupidities," I wrote, knowing that there is indeed cause for concern when Polonius gets the best notices in *Hamlet.*

Persuaded perhaps by being allowed to watch a few early rehearsals, I found Gielgud's concept of a pre-dress-rehearsal staging acceptable. I had known productions which lost ground in transition to costume, make-up, setting and lighting. But Ben Edwards's "backstage" set, while beautiful, remained a set; and Jane Greenwood's choice of "clothes," though subtle, remained costumes. Yet it is the actor who must give the true measure of any performance of *Hamlet.* Rereading my transcript of that BBC interview with Gielgud, I was aware that the director was waiting for Burton to discover his own line through the play, as he himself had done earlier with much success. Gielgud nobly refrained from forcing on this Hamlet his own Hamlet.

Unfortunately, Burton did not achieve his own Prince of Denmark—perhaps because he needed a guide, perhaps because of a lack of true seriousness, perhaps because of the distractions of the day. His was a Hamlet full of strong effective scenes made exciting by his vocal magnificence and his own sardonic personality. But his performance was no more cohesive than the *Hamlet* of Jean-Louis Barrault seen much earlier in Montreal. Barrault was at least princely, while Burton remained resolutely of the people, at least during that Toronto run.

Years later, Cronyn remembered Burton as "brilliant but uneven, " even during the long New York run which followed. He added, "We were all waiting for John's attention," indicating that none of this American cast had the confidence or experience Gielgud expected from actors. The difference between American productions of Shakespeare and the traditional British was made apparent here. This meant that, just as Torontonians flocked in search of glamour and personality, the Americans also found the Burton Hamlet very much to their taste. It broke the record that Gielgud's own Hamlet had established after breaking the one set by John Barrymore.

Toronto seemed caught up in the excitement of this try-out Hamlet, cramming the 3,200-seat house for the three weeks allotted. But when O'Keefe Centre manager Hugh Walker succeeded in getting an extra week added to the Toronto run, no box office rush resulted. Had *Hamlet* exhausted its public? Had the excitement died down so suddenly? Luckily, something appropriately newsworthy happened to resolve Walker's dilemma. With the same high level security and secrecy that had attended their weekends at Lake Simcoe, the famous lovers flew to Montreal. There, in their suite at the Ritz-Carlton Hotel, they were married by a minister from the Church of the Messiah.

The secret union could not, of course, be kept secret. In fact, news of the nuptials broke in time to start another gold rush at the O'Keefe box office. Why was this? Had part of Toronto's population withheld its patronage because the lovers were not married? Possibly, since legitimacy solved Walker's worries. The following week, Mr. and Mrs. Richard Burton left with all the furor that had brought them to town. An historic moment came after the last performance, when the Hamlet led his bride on from the wings and announced her first appearance "on any stage."

Hugh Walker recalls in his book on his O'Keefe Centre years that Burton claimed he had been in "the most costly musical in history (*Camelot*), the most expensive movie (*Cleopatra*), and the most publicized play (*Hamlet*)." Two of those events made their bows on the O'Keefe stage. And when Burton presented the Cleopatra, in person, to its audience, Toronto went wild again.

And Gielgud? In the summer of 1991, I had lunch with him at the Garrick Club in London and told him that I planned to write about his two Toronto *Hamlets*. He was preoccupied with the film *Prospero's Books,* then nearing completion. All he would tell me of the first *Hamlet* was that he had a terrible cold when it opened, and that the reflections from the glass partitions at the back of the Royal Alexandra Theatre's orchestra seating were a distraction that had to be covered. Of the O'Keefe *Hamlet*, of Richard Burton, he only smiled mysteriously and said "Ah, The Shropshire Lad Hamlet." His two *Hamlets* were in the past; he was now concerned with recording his Prospero for posterity.

Michel Saint-Denis

Born in 1897 in Beauvais, France. Educated at Collège Rollin and Lycée de Versailles. First professional work with Théâtre de Vieux-Colombier in 1912. Founded La Compagnie de Quinze in 1930. As director, staged *Noé*, *Le Viol de Lucrèce*, *Bataille de la Marne* (all by Obey). Toured with company to London in 1927. Directed *Noah (Noé)* for John Gielgud in 1935. Founded London Theatre Studio. Head of French section of BBC from 1940 to 1944. For Old Vic, directed *A Month in the Country*, *Oedipus Rex*, *Electra*. General director of Old Vic School until 1952. Founded and ran Centre National de l'Est in Strasbourg (1952-1957). Adjudicated for Dominion Drama Festival in Canada. Founder of National Theatre School of Canada in 1960; Juilliard School, Drama Division, in New York, 1969. Died in 1971.

Tyrone Guthrie

Born in Tunbridge Wells in 1900, educated at Wellington College, then at St. John's College, Oxford. First professional appearance at Oxford Playhouse, 1924. Directed Scottish National Players in 1926, followed by Festival Theatre, Cambridge. London debut with *The Anatomist* in 1931. Joined Old Vic Theatre in 1933, became administrator in 1939. Director of Company of Four, Lyric Hammersmith in 1945. To New York in 1946 to stage *He Who Gets Slapped*. Staged *Peter Grimes* at Covent Garden that year and *Cyrano de Bergerac* for the Old Vic. For Edinburgh Festival: *The Thrie Estates*, *The Gentle Shepherd. Tamburlaine the Great*, *A Midsummer Night's Dream*, *Timon of Athens* at the Old Vic. To Stratford, Ontario, in 1953 to direct *Richard III* and *All's Well That End's Well*. In Minneapolis, launched the Tyrone Guthrie Theatre. Knighted in 1961; died in 1971.

The Gifts of the Genii

At the halfway mark of the 20th century, France and Britain—our two founding nations—both sent a major genius of world theatre to Canada. Each was to grant us a golden wish and leave us with an enduring stronghold of drama: The National Theatre School and the Stratford Shakespearean Festival. Michel Saint-Denis and Tyrone Guthrie are equally revered here, though Guthrie is perhaps the better known. But back in London, where we first found them, they were recognized as complete opposites and even rivals in the early manoeuvers to establish the Royal National Theatre.

Their conflict, much exaggerated, originated during one or two of the many crucial periods at the Old Vic, cradle of the forthcoming National Theatre. Laurence Olivier, introduced to the Old Vic and to the classical stage by John Gielgud, was also indebted to him for meeting Michel Saint-Denis, a genius from France. Gielgud had imported the French director to restage André Obey's *Noah* in London in 1935. Saint-Denis's particular gift as a teacher led to the setting up of the London Theatre Studio, with financial assistance from Gielgud and Guthrie. Olivier, temporarily heading the Old Vic company, invited the roly-poly Frenchman to stage *Macbeth*. Saint-Denis's thoughtful, even plodding, approach caused the opening night to be postponed. This proved to be the last catastrophe for the Old Vic's eccentric founder, Lilian Baylis: she suffered a fatal heart attack and died before the delayed opening. Guthrie, who was to succeed her, had to be called in by Olivier to take over the unlucky production of that unlucky tragedy.

Later, in 1945, when Guthrie refused to put *Oedipus Rex* and Sheridan's *The Critic* on the same bill, Olivier brought in Saint-Denis to direct Sophocles' play, with John Piper designing. It won Olivier and the Old Vic the greatest praise at home and abroad. By then, the triumvirate of Olivier, Ralph Richardson and Saint-Denis's old pupil, John Burrell, were running the Old Vic. They appointed Saint-Denis, George Devine and Glen Byam Shaw to set up a training and experimental wing, the Old Vic School.

But while Olivier was touring in Australia, the lordly board summarily dismissed both triumvirates, resenting the time that Olivier and Richardson took to make their livings in films. Guthrie was sent for again. Saint-Denis, deeply hurt, left the country he had served so well—he had been given a CBE for his work with Free French radio during the war years—and returned to France. There, he set up another training centre, the Centre Dramatique de I'Est, at Strasbourg, with Pierre Lefevre as second-in-command.

Saint-Denis and Guthrie, so opposite in their genius for the theatre, had one thing in common. Both knew something about and were in deep sympathy with the struggle to establish a working theatre in Canada. Both had served here with honour. There was even greater honour to come.

William Tyrone Guthrie discovered Canada first, back in 1929 when he himself was twenty-nine. He kept his eye on it ever after. He had directorial successes at the Scottish National Theatre and The Playhouse in Cambridge behind him by then, but his most profitable credit was his work in radio drama. This had even attracted the attention of the Canadian National Railway, looking for a radio series that would help Canadians appreciate their own history (and, presumably, their rail transportation). After an exchange by telephone, the CNR sent its brass to England to check out the young Irish-Scot director who had made a name for himself at the British Broadcasting Corporation. The CNR project was explained. The company had already hired Merrill Denison to write *The Romance of Canada*, a series of radio dramatizations. It now needed someone with expertise to produce and edit them.

Guthrie, always attracted to faraway challenges, could fit Canada into his schedule. That is how the country attracted one of its great theatrical benefactors. Likewise, Guthrie discovered Canada—not only Montreal, where the broadcasts emanated from, but also the rest of the country—courtesy of CNR. He liked what he saw, especially the idea that this vast land could be linked together by radio drama. He made some lasting friends on his trans-Canada jaunt—people such as John Coulter, Rupert Caplan, and Dora Mavor Moore.

Guthrie kept in touch with them all, and they with him, informing him of Canada's yearnings for a theatre of its own. John Coulter, in particular, persisted in that cause, inviting him back when there was talk of a national theatre or when he'd written an epic Canadian play titled *Riel*. Guthrie knew Mrs. Moore as a cousin of his Scottish friend, James Mavor Bridie, who had alerted her that his tall friend was due. She was to be heard from again, as was Rupert Caplan, a Montrealer who had worked with Eugene O'Neill at the Provincetown Playhouse. And Merrill Denison, who was to be exhausted by Guthrie's drive for more and more radio dramas. Denison told a

Guthrie biographer, James Forsyth, that he remembered Guthrie sketching his ideas for an ideal Shakespearean theatre on napkins in a Montreal cafe between rehearsals at the Kingshall Building in 1930 or 1931.

Guthrie paid another visit to Canada ten years later, after he had staged *He Who Gets Slapped* in New York for the Theater Guild. He and his wife Judy, whom he had married in 1931, stopped over in Kingston, Ontario to spend Christmas with Robertson and Brenda Davies, friends from their days together at the Old Vic. Forsyth reports that Guthrie was talking even then about a beautiful tent theatre for Canada: "a potential sphere for future operations," as Forsyth put it.

Michel Saint-Denis first knew Canada when he was the adjudicator for the 1936 finals of the Dominion Drama Festival. He was there at the suggestion of a previous judge of some distinction, Harley Granville-Barker, friend and collaborator of George Bernard Shaw. Granville-Barker knew that Quebec was displeased with the Festival's previous choices as judges—himself excepted—all supposedly bilingual Englishmen. There was frequently a language difficulty. One adjudicator had the effrontery to proclaim that there was no decent Parisian French heard in Canada: the natives spoke a patois resembling that of 17th century France.

Granville-Barker's choice was impeccable. Born in 1897, Saint-Denis was a nephew of Jacques Copeau, the innovative founder of the Vieux-Colombier. Saint-Denis became an assistant to his uncle there and at Copeau's theatre school in Burgundy. Later, he became director of a much admired, much travelled group, La Compagnie des Quinze, which took him to London where he started a whole new career in 1935.

Both French and English competitors at Canada's

DDF approved of Saint-Denis, perhaps partly because he kowtowed to no faction. On that first visit, he awarded the top honour, the Bessborough Trophy, to the Eaton Masquers of Toronto for their staging of John Coulter's *The House in the Quiet Glen.* This gave a needed boost to Canadian playwrights in the national competition. Ottawa's Le Caveau came in second, as winner of the best play in "the opposite language."

"The opposite language" did not stay happy for long. There were rumbles in Montreal, which could be interpreted as the first signs of separatism. As director of an obscure Pushkin entry, I myself bore a message from the DDF's Montreal governors to administrators in Winnipeg, where the finals were being held in the Festival's first move out of Ottawa. The Montreal demand was that there be two Festivals—one in English, the other in French. Back came the message to Prince Paul Lieven, chairman of the Montreal contingent, echoing the Festival's Colonel Henry Osborne: "The bilingual character of our country is part of our national heritage." Osborne had the official backing of the Festival's founder, the Earl of Bessborough, who was married to a French wife and fully aware of the linguistic duality of the country to which he had been named Governor General. (My Pushkin play, oddly enough, was called *Festival in Time of Plague.*)

Saint-Denis's role in Canadian theatre was not just that of keeping its two language communities happy, although he himself became deeply involved in the struggle to see that the Bessborough proclamation of a bilingual, bicultural Festival was enforced. He was the great favourite among the Festival's adjudicators, and was affectionately called "the teacher." In Calgary, Halifax, Toronto and Saint John, he was welcomed as a judge who could inspire as well as criticize. It was in New Brunswick in

1950 that talk about a closer connection for him with Canada arose.

The years before that had found English and French Canadians separated by some concerns and united by other events during the Second World War. The Festival closed down its national competition from 1940 to 1947. Then, to pursue the Bessborough policy, Saint-Denis was invited again but was not available. When the competition was resumed, the DDF came up with its first Canadian adjudicator, Professor Emrys Jones of Saskatchewan. As had so many of the English adjudicators, he found the work of the Quebec companies most impressive. He awarded the Bessborough Trophy to *Le Medecin Malgré Lui*, staged brilliantly for Les Compagnons de Laurent by Père Emile Legault, assigned to it by his order of Holy Cross. Les Compagnons might have repeated their win the following year but Robert Speaight, whose French was most acceptable, ruled out their entry on the suspicion of clerical censorship. London's *Saint Joan* took top honours.

At this point, an odd reversal was observed. The new breed of English-Canadian actors—their professional status nervously established by CBC radio, summer stock, Dora Mavor Moore's New Play Society in Toronto, and Amelia Hall's Canadian Repertory Theatre in Ottawa—were disdaining competition with the DDF amateurs. The French-language professionals had no such compunction. They eyed the cash prizes—introduced when the Calvert Distilleries took over the top award in return for financing the DDF—as a test of their professional skills.

When Vincent Massey's report led to the establishment of the arts-supportive Canada Council, an exploratory conference held in Kingston in 1957 decided non-professional theatre was not entitled to subsidy, save to hire directors. This proved a blow to the thirty-five year old DDF and its cherished plans of a national theatre school. The honour of establishing that went to the newly formed Canadian Theatre Centre, with David Gardner as its vice president and acting chairman. Ironically, Gardner was a graduate of Hart House Theatre, run by Robert Gill, as were William Hutt, Kate Reid, Charmion King and Ted Follows. They had all competed in the Central Ontario Drama Festival, the DDF regional body in Toronto. The men also moonlighted for the University Alumnae Dramatic Club, along with John Colicos, William Needles and Richard Easton. So did I.

In 1950, various members of the DDF executive had met with Saint-Denis in Saint John, New Brunswick, to make an offer. London's Dr. Alan Skinner and William Hogg, Vancouver's Dorothy Somerset, and Toronto's Roy Stewart invited him to stay on for at least a year; $10,000 was offered. Regrettably, the offer came when Saint-Denis's career in London had collapsed and he, crushed, decided to retreat to Strasbourg. Since Saint-Denis was essential to the training plans, the matter was laid to rest for five years.

At much the same time, a Canadian offer to Guthrie found him more than receptive: he was prepared. John Coulter advised him to "investigate what was going on in Stratford." Coulter happened to be over in London and forwarded Dora Mavor Moore's appeal on behalf of Tom Patterson, who had dreamed up the concept of a Shakespearean festival in his home town of Stratford, Ontario. This proved very much more to Guthrie's taste than serving the treacherous Old Vic masters. Here was a chance to escape from backstage machinations in London and to break new ground in a country he already had warm feelings toward. His quick response to the Stratford proposal, his swift assessment of what was required, and his extraordinary gift for arousing enthusiasm for theatre where no theatre had been before were public miracles. His dynamic approach was just what staid Ontario needed to assemble a first-rate company of actors and technicians and to raise a great tent for them to play in.

Nobody else could have done that. Guthrie's great theatricality allayed any fears that classical theatre would be merely uplifting and therefore heavy going. Coupling Guthrie's vigour and experience to Tom Patterson's innocence made for an irresistible enterprise. If miracles are defined as the affirmation of faith, then the Stratford Festival was the miracle of Canada's rather disappointing century. As an early reporter of the enterprise and the first critic of their Festival, I could indeed bear witness to Tony Guthrie's messianic force in achieving it.

There is a curious link between this great event and the return of Michel Saint-Denis to fulfill his destiny here. A major offshoot of the Stratford Festival was The Canadian Players, the travelling troupe run by Douglas Campbell and Tom Patterson. After it had expanded its itinerary to include American colleges, it was operated by Tom's wife, Robin Patterson, and Laurel Crosbie. Seeking directors abroad, they contacted Saint-Denis. He declined their invitation, but indicated he was interested in the old DDF training scheme. Robin communicated this to me and I phoned Pauline McGibbon, one-time DDF president and later Lieutenant Governor of Ontario. We rallied members of the DDF executive, the Crest Theatre's Davis family, and other interested parties. Soon, with Roy Stewart as chairman, plans for theatre training in Canada were being made again.

Setting up the National Theatre School (NTS) of Canada, the result of that communiqué, was as painstaking and time-consuming as Guthrie's new enterprise was fast and eventful. Both overcame remarkable crises in financing. What had been planned as a year of varied instruction soon developed into a major institution for theatrical preparation. There was input from many people, including the Governor General himself, Vincent Massey, who thought the school should locate in Ottawa. The Montreal members of the committee, including myself, backed Saint-Denis's insistence that only in Quebec would the two theatrical cultures exist side by side.

There was also input by people who were quite unsuspecting. The Juilliard School of Music had invited Saint-Denis to set up a theatre wing, which the Rockefellers were interested in supporting. When Saint-Denis flew from France to New York, they paid his fare. We took the opportunity of flying him on to Toronto; Flora, Lady Eaton, benefactor of The Canadian Players, paid the extra fare. It has always tickled me that Saint-Denis's Canadian school opened its doors a good decade before his Juilliard School of Drama.

So Canada's two major theatre institutions appeared on our horizon mid-century, each blessed with an extraordinary leader. Those of us who could observe their great work first hand marvelled at how two such different personalities could contribute so much to our national benefit. Guthrie, the explosive genius, whipped up major classical theatre in a place where none had existed, and gave it an international reputation. Saint-Denis, philosopher and teacher nonpareil, laid the foundations for a training program that serves this country coast to coast and contributes to national unity in a unique fashion.

I have special memories of both men, as have so many people in Canada. Of Guthrie, I remember his tall person ushering me out of Stratford's very first rehearsal, which I had hoped to record. "No place for the press!" he declared. Recognizing my deep disappointment, he softened the expulsion by adding, "Come to lunch." He knew that I cared.

The sharp commands and the resounding hand-claps which characterized his directorial technique suggested that Dr. Guthrie was a dictator, and in some ways he was. But he could also ask opinions of others. I think he trusted me because I knew what he was aiming for—a theatre such as William Poel might have dreamed of, communicative without being scenic, serving the plays rather than the individual actors.

When I found his splendid production of *Tamburlaine* too long, he took me up to the highest place in the Royal Alexandra Theatre for a matinee performance and thrust at me his copy of Marlowe's soaring work. "What would you cut?" he challenged. I could find few lines. But I was immensely flattered.

I was even more impressed when Guthrie allowed me to report on his rehearsals for *Hamlet*, which opened the new Guthrie Theatre in Minneapolis, after Mary Joliffe, press agent par excellence, spoke up for me. It was intoxicating to watch the great man in action, to witness how he achieved the performance, the pictures and the pace to make Shakespeare's signature play new.

A guard was instructed to faint at one point to accentuate a moment of high tension. "Do it again!" commanded the voice behind me. The soldier did so. Then Guthrie dropped down behind my chair. "Is that too distracting?" he asked. I thought that it was, but I answered cautiously: "Not the second time." He was breathing hard, having been constantly on the move through the new amphitheatre. George Grizzard as the Prince, Jessica Tandy as Gertrude, old Montreal friend Hume Cronyn as

Polonius—all were wonderfully responsive to their great director, for whom this theatre was named.

Of Michel Saint-Denis my fondest memory is sharing an afternoon visit to his modest chateau in France. I recall the old man of theatre bending to listen to his one-time radio pupil from the days in England, Charles de Gaulle, who was proposing a constitution for France's Fifth Republic. Puffing on his pipe, Michel listened not so much to the General's message to "le tout France" as to his pupil's delivery of it.

Both Suria Saint-Denis and Judy Guthrie have their special places in my memory of some wonderful times, but one more memory will wind this up. On a sunny day in Stratford, I came across a Montreal member of the company, Leo Ciceri, giving a movement class to visiting NTS students. To compensate for the decision to locate in Montreal, the NTS board had allowed for one summer term to be held annually in Stratford. There, in the Stratford sunshine, the spirit of the two world-theatre men combined and commingled with Canada's two founding nations represented by bright young students—in a pleasant Ontario town with a world-theatre reputation.

Postscript

That erudite critic, Professor Ronald Bryden of The Drama Centre at the University of Toronto, researching his book on Guthrie, uncovered evidence of some pointed ridicule in Guthrie's relationship with Saint-Denis. Guthrie could be magnificently scathing on occasion, but Saint-Denis was not capable of sharpness or criticism. Philip Hope-Wallace once found himself adjudicating for the DDF with Saint-Denis in the front row: "I felt like an RSPCA inspector suddenly confronted by St. Francis of

Assisi." (Hope-Wallace also recognized that Saint-Denis "played a valuable role in a land bedevilled with the problems of a bilingual culture.")

The CBC Radio Drama department under Esse Ljungh invited Saint-Denis to give a lecture/demonstration at the Crest Theatre in 1958. There, he hailed Guthrie as "a great example of intellectual curiosity combined with practical resources," going on to praise his "show of brilliance of pageantry. No theatre," he declared, "could compare with the Festival Theatre at Stratford." Then he added delicately, "One side of Shakespeare in any case."

Saint-Denis's impassioned disciples were more critical, Bryden says. His former student, Powys Thomas—first head of the English Section of the National Theatre School—was indiscreet enough to make fun of Guthrie's contrasting methods during that last summer term at Stratford, an environment passionately dedicated to the genius of Guthrie. Bryden claims it was this ridicule that led to the severance of the connection between Guthrie's festival and Saint-Denis's school. However, we original board members of the school, who had advocated Stratford's summer term, were just told that the increasing expense of billeting students was the reason for breaking this historic link.

Edward Gordon Craig

International stage innovator, born near London in 1872. Educated at Bradfield and Heidelberg colleges. Started acting career in 1885 with Henry Irving and Ellen Terry, his mother. Progressed to Shakespearean leads, including Hamlet (1897). Began career as designer in 1898 with two Purcell operas followed by productions for Ellen Terry, Eleonora Duse and Constantin Stanislavsky. Publications include *On the Art of Theatre* (1911), *Towards a New Theatre* (1915), *The Theatre Advances* (1921), *Books and Theatres* (1925) plus a magazine, *The Mask*, as well as biographies of Irving and Terry. Died in 1966.

A Sword Flashing

The Associated Designers of Canada may not take it kindly that their first honorary member fails to include any Canadians in this recollection of world-theatre designers. There are many of their members today of sufficient status—artists such as Stratford's Susan Benson, the Shaw Festival's Cameron Porteous, and others from Robert Prevost to Michael Levine. But I have elected to discuss three visiting artists of whom I have had personal acquaintance: the great Tanya Moiseiwitsch, Robert Edmond Jones and Edward Gordon Craig. (The adjective, of course, is shared by all three.)

I could not catalogue world-theatre personalities without reference to this particular field of stage artistry, because this has long been a passion of mine. I entered theatre as a designer, creating costumes and stage pictures for The Everyman Players at the Church of the Messiah in Montreal. Tipped off about the group by old Strathcona Academy school friends, I stayed with them for eight years of church productions, including Shaw's *Saint Joan*, Claudel's *Tidings Brought to Mary* and Eliot's *Murder in the Cathedral*. One original work, *The Spanish Miracle* by George Brewer, founder of the group, allowed me to stage a whole show "after El Greco," whom I had just discovered.

Gordon Craig's inspiration came early but indirectly, when I was taken to His Majesty's in Montreal to see Sir

John Martin-Harvey play Hamlet in a production which he had based on Craig's concepts of design. Martin-Harvey and Craig had both been beginners in the great company of Sir Henry Irving, "Teddy" Craig having the advantage of being the adored son of Irving's leading lady, Ellen Terry. The two juveniles discussed their ambitions to stage their own productions of the classics in their own ways. Craig's productions were wildly visionary, and shocked young Martin-Harvey, as they shocked the world later.

But Martin-Harvey was fascinated. He recognized the Craig genius in practical terms when he came to tour his own *Hamlet* decades later. He even invited Craig to direct it. Craig would not have been at all interested in the first Martin-Harvey staging, which was 11th century archeological in the fashion of the day. But when he toured *Hamlet* abroad, Martin-Harvey drew upon Craig's concepts. Soaring curtains replaced the stone painted walls. A great cyclorama backed every scene, with a low rising silhouette of battlements at its base, save where the sunken crosses of a graveyard were needed. A truly poetic production. I was entranced by it at the age of twelve, and made paper models of its scenes. I also made the connection with Craig—or rather S. Morgan-Powell of *The Montreal Star* made it for me—and thereafter I read all I could about this truly legendary artist.

Morgan-Powell set me on a path of inspiration, so I was startled when I came across Martin-Harvey's account of his travelling *Hamlet*. In his autobiography, he gave more credit for his inspiration to Max Reinhardt than he did to Craig. In particular, he traced the soaring skies of the design to Reinhardt's use of a plaster cyclorama, or "horizon" as he called it. (He quite rejected Robert Edmond Jones's permanent setting for the Barrymore *Hamlet*; great visionaries do not always share the same great vision.)

Martin-Harvey certainly gave credit to his former fellow-player in Irving's company for his later influence on Duse, Granville-Barker, Stanislavsky and, incidentally, Reinhardt. But he was miffed when Craig turned down his invitation to direct his *Hamlet*, especially by the suggestion that it be directed by one of Craig's pupils. Craig, on the other hand, resented Martin-Harvey's invitation to the German director to stage *Oedipus Rex* for him in London. That was why he had given the cold shoulder to the *Hamlet* invitation. But reconciliation had evidently been achieved when Sir John was interviewed later by Morgan-Powell—a meeting of accumulated hyphens.

I detected Craig's influence everywhere, including Douglas Fairbanks's film of *Robin Hood*. How I yearned to emulate him, but vast cycloramas proved difficult in the theatres I was designing for. I had one made up of parachute silk for my first *Lear*, but backlighting it was hard to accomplish. My small stage in the Church of the Messiah led me more comfortably to the theories of William Poel, yet I still dreamed of soaring towers and deep skies.

I wonder if the child Craig had ever glimpsed the prairie landscapes when touring with Irving or seen the low horizons and towering grain elevators of the Canadian West. A more tangible connection with that landscape was to emerge elsewhere.

In 1908, Craig received his most famous commission: to design a *Hamlet* for the Moscow Art Theatre (MXAT).

There, he was to work closely with Constantin Stanislavsky's right-hand man—his closest friend, associate director Leopold Sulerzhitsky, who had some unique memories of Canada. A practical man as well as an artist, he had been sent by another friend, Count Leo Tolstoy, to organize and settle into that Canadian landscape an outcast sect, the Doukhobors. He became their *tolstrogan*, their leader in establishing an ideal community. When he returned to join forces with Stanislavsky, the latter was planning a theatre that was also to be an actors' commune. "Sulerzhitsky and I dreamed of creating a spiritual order of actors. Its members were to be men and women of broad and uplifted views or wide horizons and ideas," wrote Stanislavsky.

To this vision of wide horizons, Sulerzhitsky added his Canadian experience. He "brought the real poetry of the prairies," as his new friend Stanislavsky described it. He was put in charge of the communal home for actors eventually set up for the MXAT company in the Crimean countryside. Sulerzhitsky supervised the actors in Moscow, leading the exercises Stanislavsky devised for his famous "method"—relaxing the muscles first, then attaining truth and belief through improvisation. Stanislavsky also entrusted to his friend "Suler" a guest—that great genius of theatre, Gordon Craig.

The guest proved one of the most difficult of his responsibilities, for Craig was working out many of his theories for the first time. Their Moscow collaboration offers us diametric opposites in theatre philosophies of the 20th century—supreme artists, each searching for his truth. Sulerzhitsky finally withdrew under the strain, to nobody's amazement but with much distress. "A great artist," Sulerzhitsky explained; "that he is our guest, I also know. I can put up with the rudeness, irritability and confusion of this man . . . and still be fond of him." Their biggest difference came when Sulerzhitsky objected to the darkness Craig imposed on "the mouse-trap scene." But when Craig cut Sulerzhitsky's name off the program, that was too much. The familiar duo—the English artist with flowing hair and scarf and borrowed furs, discussing with the shorter Sulerzhitsky in his duck-tailed Canadian coat and buckwheat hat, mixing languages and laughter—was to be seen no more.

Years later, in 1961, when my shelves were heavy with books on Craig, I received an astonishing invitation from Broadway producer and friend Oliver Rea, to visit the grand figure of theatre design. Rea and I were staying on the Cote d'Azur, and Craig had retired to nearby Vence, where he was attended by his daughter, Nelly, whom I recall as somewhat disapproving.

In the bright sunshine which bathed his white cottage, Craig was most outgoing—a fine aquiline profile white-topped like a great bird. Here was the illegitimate son of Edward Godwin and Ellen Terry. As a child he had been brought to North America in the company of Henry Irving, who had given the lad every encouragement for his mother's sake. (Craig had been saluted for his youthful beauty by Oscar Wilde in a letter which his mother intercepted. She need not have worried, for young Craig was attracted early to the opposite sex, marrying into it often.) The opportunities he was given as actor (Martin-Harvey, though older, was his understudy) influenced him less than Irving's mastery of staging—a great inspiration to insurrection.

Good enough to have played Hamlet twice himself, Craig's greatest fame came when he was invited by Stanislavsky to create a production of that play for the Moscow Art Theatre. His visit to Russia was enhanced by his love affair with Isadora Duncan. Perhaps that distraction played its part in the disaster of opening night, when the towering screens Craig designed toppled out of control of the MXAT stage crew. But this catastrophe didn't destroy his reputation as a great innovator of theatre—well bolstered by the literature as well as the drawings, etchings, woodcuts and models with which he illustrated his theories.

We spent a wonderful afternoon in Vence that summer's day in 1961. As journalist Hallie Flanaghan discovered in her 1928 interview with him in Copenhagen, where he was staging Ibsen's *The Pretenders*, "To attempt to record the conversation of Gordon Craig is to attempt to describe a sword flashing." It still held true. "No, there was nobody like Irving," he declared. Then he recounted a long ago moment when the great actor/manager forgave him some youthful misdemeanour on stage in *The Corsican Brothers*.

What other actors had he admired? "The Italians," he enthused. "Acting comes easily to them. Grasso, for instance, made his entrance as Othello crawling on his hands and knees. Of course it was too much, but he got away with it. Eleanor Duse? My mother looked up to her. Impossible woman, though. Thought she was right up at the top. And she was."

What of the French? Of Duse's great rival, Sarah Bernhardt? Craig laughed. "Adorable, impossible. Last time I saw her—Yvette Guilbert took me to see her—she was very old and a bit . . . you know. Well, do you know what she asked me? She said, 'How is Irving?' And Irving had been dead 12 years by then. I told her that I thought he was doing very well where he was. 'Still keeps at it, does she?' she asked."

Gaston Baty was someone he had liked among the French actors. And Louis Jouvet, who was his friend—"not a great actor, but a great producer." Baty, Jouvet and Charles Dullin—"as an actor, a little like his name."

Of course, we spoke of Martin-Harvey and the *Hamlet* based on Craig's concepts. He was tolerant of his old comrade in arms: "all those curtains and gauzes!" The great artist who had revolutionized the 19th century stage with his sweeping and very striking draperies as well as rare use of light and shadow now dismissed the things which were the trademarks of his designs!

They were only means to an end, he implied—a simplicity which is achieved finally in a theatre like Stratford's festival theatre or the then projected Guthrie Theatre in Minneapolis. "That's in the United States, isn't it?" he asked Oliver Rea, who had joined forces with Tyrone Guthrie and Tanya Moiseiwitsch to create the Guthrie Theatre there. I was very proud to have introduced them.

Craig also spoke well of Bernard Miles's Mermaid Theatre in London. "If only I'd been given my own theatre in London," he lamented, "I would have done such things!" But there was no bitterness left as he balanced his enjoyment of the present with the past. Rather, he wanted to see the plans for Minneapolis and the changes in Stratford, Ontario.

"That fellow Guthrie's clever," he said, "but why

doesn't he come and see me? The others come, Bernard Miles comes to stay, and that fellow Peter Brook comes to see me." When we were leaving, it was "Keep in touch! When you write, remind me who you are and when you came. I often forget!" And he waived from his deck chair—that bright old genius—as the car swung round and down the hillside from Vence.

I sent him my *Globe* piece when I got home. His response is dated September 16, 1961. "Dear Mr. Whittaker," went this beautifully placed wander of words: "Thank you for sending me the 'interview' I think its excellent. This is only a bare scrap of a note to say 'thanks' Yours sincerely Gordon Craig."

Another card dated earlier but arriving later reads: "Dear Mr. Whittaker I was glad to hear from you and that you found in me a human being I am not a mere wooden signpost pointing 'this way and that way out' All good luck to you and always let me hear from friends Yours sincerely Gordon Craig." Along the side of the card is written: "remember me to Mr. Rea 'the short one'!" And on the back of the card is a P.S. which reads: "erase scribble my cat will everlastingly jump on my board as I write my notes and letters. Blessed white cat—and I can't be cross with her," he adds forgivingly. In his son's book about him, Craig is quoted from this period. "Few visitors call—all the better—but one or two are enough. It's a queer age, ninety-two is. My white pussy cat is a joy. Never a harsh word—always loving—looks at me. . . ." The word "looks" was underlined.

Further reminder of that wonderful visit for me was Craig's willingness, even eagerness, to sign his picture to "the short one" and "the tall one." The picture he signed was a copy of a sketch of him, signed L. Pasternak, dating back to those historic days in Moscow. Craig identified it as being done by "the father of that chap they murdered in Russia the other day." Novelist Boris Pasternak had died just recently. It appeared that Craig at ninety had kept up connections with the Russians of his great days there.

Robert Edmond Jones

Born in New Hampshire in 1887. A designer, director and producer. Studied at Harvard, then with Max Reinhardt in Berlin. Professional designer in 1915 for Harley Granville-Barker on *The Man Who Married a Dumb Wife*; *Til Eulenspiegel*, with Nijinsky, in 1916. With Kenneth MacGowan, managed Greenwich Village Playhouse. For Arthur Hopkins and John Barrymore, designed *Richard III* in 1920; *Hamlet* in 1922. Designed and directed Eugene O'Neill's *Anna Christie* in 1921; also designed O'Neill's *Desire Under the Elms*, *Mourning Becomes Electra* for Broadway. Other productions designed: *Lucrece* with Katharine Cornell in 1932; *Othello* with Paul Robeson in 1936; *The Philadelphia Story* with Katharine Hepburn in 1939; *Lute Song* in 1946. Worked in colour for films, including *Becky Sharp* in 1935. Books include *Continental Stagecraft* with Kenneth MacGowan, 1922; *Drawings for the Theatre*, 1925; *The Dramatic Imagination*, 1941. Died in 1954.

A Visionary in the Camp

I had many opportunities to see and appreciate Robert Edmond Jones's highly poetic designs for New York theatre in the magazine called *Theatre Arts,* once the Bible of all remote disciples of the stage. I also had an opportunity to see first-hand his stunning setting for "Mephistopheles' Serenade" in *Faust*, as toured by the innovative American Opera Company to Montreal's Princess Theatre. Later, his settings for the famous production of *Othello* that Margaret Webster directed for Paul Robeson were seen in Montreal at His Majesty's. Between these, reproductions of his were often published—most famously those for the John Barrymore *Richard III*, the *Hamlet* also with Barrymore, and Eugene O'Neill's *Mourning Becomes Electra.*

The Canadian Army became interested in Jones's ideas for troop entertainment, and the Auxiliary Services, Camp Supervisors, invited him to Canada. Jones believed that, instead of depending on the professional concert parties that toured around the camps, the army should entertain itself. He advocated the organization of self-entertainment, with the men contributing their own talent, no matter how untrained: "The ocarina, old familiar songs, recitations, burlesques, pratfalls."

I don't know if Canada's military followed up Jones's theories with The Army Show or put them into practice to any extent; but attention was certainly paid to them by *The Gazette,* which ran a two column story under the heading, "A Visionary in the Camp," establishing Jones as a theatre man of importance. I had written the article myself, being by then the junior in *The Gazette*'s entertainment department, as well as an aspiring stage designer. The piece, which showed my considerable knowledge of Jones's Broadway work, drew from him a letter of appreciation (and perhaps some astonishment), concluding with an invitation to call him if ever I were in New York.

Free railway passes when I was working for the Canadian Pacific Railway had taken me to New York on holidays; and they were also available to *Gazette* employees on occasion. I made sure that my next holiday took me to New York and to Mr. Jones's studio. He was pleased to discover that I was an aspiring designer myself, and followed up our discussions with an invitation to dine at The Players Club, prestigious rendezvous for New York theatre folk.

Where Gordon Craig's influence was international—with only his native England resisting—Robert Edmond Jones's impact was local, concentrating on one theatrical centre. But what a centre! He worked almost exclusively for New York's Broadway stage.

After the First World War, the cross-section of entertainment at the heart of the great metropolis burst into activity that became recognized internationally. When George M. Cohan, an entertainer of unusual energy and virtuosity, sang, "Give My Regards to Broadway," he was sticking the label on a unique concentration of activity. From that entertainment capital, touring companies carried forth the latest New York hits. Everything began there and emanated from there.

Jones resented the pace Broadway imposed on creativity. "The scene designer is forced to work and think in a hundred different ways—now as a dressmaker, now as a sculptor, now as a jeweller," he wrote in *The New York Times*. And again: "Insufficient time is generally allowed for the pre-rehearsal creative planning in the theatre. . . . I firmly believe that there is no clear demarcation between the planning phase of the director's work and the creative plan of a good designer's job." To which Jones added: "The ideal would be a director with the facilities to do his own designing—and enough time."

He himself achieved that on more than one occasion, the most notable being *Anna Christie* in 1921. It was a triumph for him and Pauline Lord, and it won O'Neill the Pulitzer Prize that year. He opposed Broadway's realism to the end—as an imposition by Hollywood—and attacked its failure to enlarge its vision. "Why is it that the theatre . . . so persistently avoids the possibility of any contagion from the other arts?" he asked.

Broadway grew out of a mix of vaudeville, burlesque, ethnic expression, and attempts to recreate the more dignified theatres of Europe. These succeeded until the imported farces and comedies were no longer needed and its own fare proved something highly original. Broadway reflected America and, in turn, America reflected Broadway.

Naturally, Broadway looked for its own playwrights and found them—even if it didn't trust them as crowd pleasers, employing play-doctors to polish their output. Broadway producers emerged as experts in crowd pleasing, yet they weren't all cigar-chomping showmen. Some gentlemen of wealth and taste found public recognition on Broadway.

In time, the product was uplifted. The Theatre Guild brought new importance to Broadway. Serious plays were legitimized by the Pulitzer Prizes as moral. America was reflected on stage. The conventional box set and footlights soon vanished, as did the old scene painters and carpenters responsible for the look of a show. The era of the designer arrived—Lee Simonson, Jo Mielziner, Donald Oenslager, Frank Brangwyn, Norman Bel Geddes, Mordecai Gorlik. But the most revered of all designers was Robert Edmond Jones—for his poetic vision and his association with productions of high distinction. His partnership with Arthur Hopkins, which was to make a classical actor out of John, antic younger son of the Barrymore family, was a case in point. Jones revered Barrymore's talent: first Tolstoy's *Redemption*, then Shakespeare's *Richard III* and then *Hamlet*, after which Hollywood stole Barrymore to be another star in its own sky.

At the Players Club, Jones gazed at the portrait of Barrymore's Hamlet with deep affection. "When Gielgud took the skull of Yorick, it was the cue for a great speech. When Barrymore took it, it was the skull of an old friend."

Jones's tribute to John Barrymore was but one recollection of that memorable visit. I was awed by the towering portrait of the actor Edwin Booth by John Singer Sargent, which seemed so right in its place over the Players Club's fireplace, the club's founder stretched to godlike proportions. (I knew height was not one of that famous Hamlet's assets.) Then the gathering of Broadway stalwarts for drinks made me feel very much in the centre of American theatre, with Mr. Jones as my mentor. I remember his description of playwright Lillian Hellman and her producer, Herman Shumlin, at work. "First Lillian climbs up the rock face, putting spikes in. Then comes Shumlin, moving ahead of her, adding more spikes. First one, then the other, all the way to the top. At no time has either of them turned to appreciate the landscape! I hate Lillian Hellman, and I wish she were dead!" Not the person, the playwright.

My ears perked up when Mr. Jones mentioned Margaret Anglin, the esteemed Canadian actress then at the end of her career yet still hoping to continue work. "I've suggested she stick to radio acting," he explained when a comment was made about her becoming fat. "Now as round about as she is tall," he added. Then he made a gesture of bending the elbow, being too gentle a soul to explain further the cause of her added weight.

Turning to design, Jones spoke expressively, signifying a concentration of light, colour, glory, strength and beauty without necessarily using any of those words. We went on to talk of his famous *Othello* and I was startled to discover that he had not approved of the casting of Paul Robeson opposite Uta Hagen. It smacked of sensationalism to him, a stern New Englander still. He remembered the director Margaret Webster as "Peggy, a sort of dragoon moving around giving orders."

We disagreed on the then current scandal of the Windsors. He disapproved of the Duke and conjured up an image to support it. "It was at a princess's villa in Nice, converted to a sort of hotel. There in the midst of a crowd of beautiful English people in formal dress—and you know, they are beautiful—ascending the stairs is Edward, wearing only a G-string no bigger than Gypsy Rose Lee's, and pink! Walking without a care in the world up the great white marble staircase." Jones's account of this glimpse of British monarchy reminded me at the time of "The Emperor's New Clothes" described by a Puritan.

Jones spoke a great deal about his late wife, Margaret Carrington, sister of Walter Huston. It was she who taught John Barrymore to speak Shakespeare's verse. Jones spoke of her not with sadness but as if she were still living.

He mentioned Vladimir Nijinsky, who had wanted a ballet set to Liszt's "Mephisto Waltz." "When he broke with Diaghilev and came over here, I worked with him. He was a very simple person. All great people are simple. It's when you mix in the others that everything gets so complicated." Jones had worked with the great Russian dancer on his own ballet set to Richard Strauss's "Til Eulenspeigel," staged at New York's Metropolitan Opera House as a vision of fantastic mediaevalism.

He had seen not only Nijinsky but also Bernhardt—the latter when she was still beautiful. He remembered her entrance as Phèdre, supported by handmaidens. Jones himself had been discovered by the entrepreneur Morris Gest when Jones was instructing at Harvard University. Gest arranged for Jones to study abroad with the great Max Reinhardt. He came back to assist Joseph Urban on a vast *Masque of Caliban*, played to an audience of twenty thousand in Harvard Stadium.

At the opposite end of the scale, Jones worked with Eugene O'Neill at the Provincetown Playhouse and designed the famous O'Neill productions on Broadway: the great Greek portico of *Mourning Becomes Electra,* the austere New England farmhouse of *Desire Under the Elms,* the waterfront saloon of *Anna Christie,* no less poetic because it was so faithful. Also the designs for *Redemption*, *Richard III* and *Hamlet* for Arthur Hopkins and John Barrymore. And I cap these surviving designs with my own memory of his *Lute Song,* surely the most beautiful single musical in the history of Broadway.

On my wall, I treasure one of the simplest sketches Jones ever put to paper. It was the beginning of an idea for a production of Shakespeare's *Henry VIII* he was working on. A hint of high battlements against a sky; below, the suggestion of a spotlight catching a halberdier. I had picked it off his workroom floor during a later visit. He let me keep it as an example of how simply great stage pictures can illustrate great drama.

Tanya Moiseiwitsch

Born in London in 1914. Educated at Central School of Arts and Crafts. Married Felix Krish. First theatre work at Old Vic Theatre. Design debut at Westminster Theatre, followed by Abbey Theatre, Dublin; Duchess Theatre, London; Oxford Playhouse, Lyric Theatre, Hammersmith; Old Vic in Liverpool, Bristol and London's Old Vic, the latter including *Uncle Vanya*, *The Critic* and *Cyrano de Bergerac*. To Canada in 1953 to design stage and productions at Stratford Shakespearean Festival for Tyrone Guthrie. Designed twenty-nine productions there, including *Richard III*, *All's Well That Ends Well*, *Oedipus Rex*, *Henry V*, *Cymbeline*. Also worked for Edinburgh Festival, Piccolo Teatro (Milan), Royal Shakespeare Company, Royal Opera House at Covent Garden, Habima Theatre (Tel Aviv), National Theatre (London), Metropolitan Opera (New York).

The Most Silent Star

Daughter of two remarkable public figures—Benno Moiseiwitsch the pianist and his musician wife Daisy (later married to the celebrated playwright John Drinkwater)—little Tanya opted early on for a strong personal reserve. A photograph album in the Victoria and Albert Museum's theatre collection showed the company of the Malvern Festival, with Shaw himself and the Drinkwaters. Under it, her mother had written: "Where's Tanya?"

Where was Tanya indeed? Making a name for herself as a stage designer of extraordinary range, of remarkable artistry and great skill, who could follow her designs all the way through the workshops until their final vision was accomplished. Her modesty and reserve made her especially sensitive to the demands of the director, the players and the playwright. She won respect in such historic show palaces as Dublin's Abbey Theatre, England's Royal Shakespeare Company (RSC) and National Theatre, the Metropolitan Opera in New York, and, for us most importantly, the Stratford Festival of Canada.

The year before Tyrone Guthrie persuaded her to join him in Ontario to create that festival, she had prepared a remarkable production design for Shakespeare's Histories at Stratford-upon-Avon. Her concept of an all-purpose Shakespearean (but not Elizabethan and certainly not mock-Tudor) setting achieved a vision only dreamed of in England after Henry Irving's day. Scholars such as

William Poel had demonstrated how much better, and more complete, the plays could be when staged simply, dispensing with the spectacle so greatly favoured by Sir Henry and by Sir Herbert Beerbohm Tree.

Mind you, even in 1951 and under the auspices of the Shakespeare Memorial Theatre (as the RSC was then known), there were authorities who fought such new simplicity. Sir Harold Hobson, then the theatre critic for *The Times,* had difficulty. He described the "permanent setting" by Tanya Moiseiwitsch thus: "A steep and treacherous staircase ran up one side of the stage to a balcony overlooking a space in the centre, which was used indiscriminately for battles, the interior of Mistress Quickley's inn, Shallow's Gloucestershire garden, the watchfires of Agincourt, and John of Gaunt's death chamber. The advantages of this setting were, of course, a great saving of expense," said the gentleman from *The Times*, barking up the wrong tree, "and an equal gain in swiftness of transition from scene to scene," he added more perceptively. Then he veered sharply off again: "Some poetic effect might also have been expected from the contrast between the permanence of the set and the fleetingness of the men and women acting their little turbulent unhappy lives upon it."

But Sir Harold didn't think that "any such effect was attained, and as the plays progressed one felt increasingly that the dark enclosed atmosphere of stairs and balcony was inimical to any feeling of green grass and open air." Happily, Sir Harold lived to be gratified, presumably, by Olivier's film of *Henry V* bursting onto the greenness of the Irish grass for its Agincourt.

Others saw the Moiseiwitsch Histories as the fulfillment of the Poel dream. Having noticed that his Elsinore

Hamlet worked wonderfully when forced by bad weather into a hotel ballroom, Tyrone Guthrie was encouraged to fling an old Scottish play, *The Thrie Estates,* into the middle of Edinburgh's Assembly Hall, this time deliberately. He recognized the special Moiseiwitsch talent as the right design component when Tom Patterson approached him (via Dora Mavor Moore and John Coulter) to start a Shakespearean Festival in Ontario's green and pleasant countryside in 1953.

The partnership between Tyrone Guthrie and Tanya Moiseiwitsch began when Guthrie, who knew her parents and was fond of them both, invited Tanya to join the Liverpool Old Vic Company in 1944. There, he was planning to stage *The Alchemist.* When Guthrie joined the Old Vic in London, he persuaded her to become part of that exciting enterprise.

She designed two of the most admired productions at the Old Vic: the luminous Chekhovian *Uncle Vanya,* directed by John Burrell for Olivier and Richardson, and Sheridan's *The Critic,* which was part of the famous double bill with Sophocles' *Oedipus Rex* in 1945.

Guthrie had some reservations about the Sophocles play (as directed by Michel Saint-Denis) and shared them with Tanya. James Forsyth, Guthrie's biographer, explains that "he was from this moment determined somehow to do his [own] production of the play." Indeed, he was to do it memorably, in a theatre as yet unbuilt, and with his choice of designer, Tanya Moiseiwitsch.

I also had developed an affinity with the Stratford-upon-Avon Histories, having fallen into thrust stage theatre when designing *Everyman* for the Church of the Messiah in my Montreal beginnings. I carried Poel's ideas along when designing three of the plays at McGill

University's Moyse Hall for the Shakespeare Society of Montreal. So I also knew from previous experience what miracles these Moiseiwitsch Histories achieved.

I had been summoned to Stratford-upon-Avon when I arrived in London that summer by a wire from Montrealer Leo Ciceri, announcing that he was taking over the role of Ancient Pistol and expecting me to report on this event. Accompanied by Don Harron, Herman and Violet Voaden—fellow Canadian visitors—we went backstage after the performance to congratulate Ciceri on his good break. He rewarded us by introducing us to Tanya Moiseiwitsch herself. The exuberance of Leo's visitors plainly startled her, although not enough to discourage her when the offer came from Dr. Guthrie. Yet she has retained her wariness of Canadian newspapermen even when they are enthusiastic. She laughs when I claim that she covers up whatever she's working on before answering my phone calls, but the joke isn't that far-fetched.

Over the years, we have remained friendly. When a great exhibition devoted to the Moiseiwitsch designs was planned at the Stratford Art Gallery in the 40th anniversary year of the festival, it was she who reminded me that she had given me the original design for Irene Worth's costume as the doctor in that first year's *All's Well That Ends Well.* (She had even inscribed it "For Herbie.") I called the organizers of the exhibition and offered it along with "the Stratford sword" used by Alec Guinness as Richard III, suggesting both mementos be labelled "From the Collection of Herbert Whittaker, courtesy of the Theatre Museum of Ontario" for which it is destined. I missed this reminder of the great designer from my green walls—the reminder of herself, of her friendship, and of the great contribution she has made to Canada's theatre.

Although that Moiseiwitsch exhibition captured the range of designs for Stratford which this great artist had made, it could not detail all of the ways she contributed to the character of the festival and to its professionalism and craftsmanship. She set up the workshops, then taught generations of designers and costumiers how to transform a costume into a character's clothing, how to create designs that help the actors find their characters (and feel good doing so), and how to create the myriad properties that the Bard's cycle of plays demands.

That doctor's gown for Helena, for instance, is an intricacy of jersey silk worn over a black robe, allowing the actress to move with grace as she pushed Guinness along in his king's wheelchair. When Richard achieved the throne, his crimson robe covered the stage to suggest the blood he had spilled to get there. When the ladies-in-waiting to the Princess of France filled the stage in *Love's Labour's Lost,* they were all in virginal white; but each one wore a different white. The blue of the French court's armour contrasted expressively with England's earth colours in the famous *Henry V* in 1956. And so it went through the Moiseiwitsch years. Other designers were called upon as the seasons went on, but many of them seemed to be fighting the simplicity of her elegant, unpretentious, superbly proportioned stage. When they learned to give in to it, they increased significantly in stature.

The lucky ones who learned directly from her, discovered the importance of colour and its relationships. They learned what materials worked on stage and the process that transforms costumes into clothes with character and a past. They discovered that the designs with swatches attached, which inspired directors and actors, had to be accompanied by many quick sketches to instruct wardrobe workers. And that stage jewellery was never really as extravagant as it seemed.

Directors learned, too. But what they learned from Tanya, she will never tell us. She insists that she merely carried out the director's intentions for the play being worked upon. In a letter after that first season (in which she flatly refused remuneration for the design of the doctor's gown she gave me), an unintentional glimpse slipped into her report of an assignment for Giorgio Strehler, the master-director of Milan's Piccolo Teatro. The production was *Giardino dei Ciliegi,* a very Italian showing of *The Cherry Orchard.*

"Strehler is obviously a wonderful director. My one quarrel with him is his idea that all Russians must be fair. His Italian cast of dark, flashing-eyed women must be clapped into honey-coloured wigs. I pleaded with his assistant, a Spanish-speaking South American, to woo him away from that idea. . . . The Trofimov was dark but offered to dab his hair with peroxide rather than wear a wig." That may be as close as we'll come to Tanya Moiseiwitsch admitting she had tried to influence any director. So we must believe that all directorial talents she has worked with inherited a brilliant visual sense—temporarily at least.

As designers, actors and directors learned to submit to the magic of this great thrust stage, audiences at the Stratford Festival continue to draw comfort from its proportions. To settle into our seats before it is to succumb to its drawing power. The whole auditorium centres on that stage, thrust modestly forward to carry the action of the evening. It is at its best when at its simplest. I dream back to that *Love's Labour's Lost* in 1961. An old vine climbed the central pillar to the upper stage; the openings then above the side doors were heavy with great old volumes. Without anything else added, the setting and theme of the play were established for us.

When Michael Langham asked for certain changes in Moiseiwitsch's design—"to make it more masculine," somebody said—its original design accommodated them perfectly, under her watchful eye. When fellow designer Leslie Hurry added Druidic stone shapes for the Langham *Lear*, they were discarded as the final rehearsals progressed. The original Moiseiwitsch stage carried the greatest of tragedies as it did the most elegant of comedies. It is a stage for all seasons, created by a genius of stage design.

That most loving exhibition—Tanya Moiseiwitsch: Designs for Stratford—consecrated this major contribution to Canadian theatre. But any complete tribute to the designer as a figure of importance in world theatre—which Moiseiwitsch undoubtedly is, in the noble line of Gordon Craig and Robert Edmond Jones—must at least touch on her outside triumphs such as that first *Peter Grimes* for Covent Garden (repeated for the Metropolitan Opera in New York) or the more recent *La Traviata* for the Met. Considered together, the "abstract expressionism" of the Britten premiere balanced the astonishing handling of space in the Verdi classic.

I have mentioned the famous Histories at Stratford-upon-Avon in 1951, and the wonderfully contrasted *Uncle Vanya* and *The Critic* in that 1945-46 old Vic program. But there are many others that must at least be mentioned: Ralph Richardson's *Cyrano de Bergerac* for the Old Vic in 1944, the *Othello* which Stratford-upon-Avon took to Australia and New Zealand in 1952, Tyrone Guthrie's great success with *The Matchmaker* (which started out in Edinburgh), that other Thornton Wilder work, *A Life in the Sun* (which began and ended there), and *The Merchant of Venice* for the Habima, surely a landmark production. She also costumed Olivier's last *Lear* for television.

To quote from the apt words of Elliot Hayes in the catalogue to that 1992 exhibition: "Moiseiwitsch sculpted theatrical space. Working with Guthrie, she influenced the production of Shakespeare in this century as no designer before or since." We Canadians expand with pride in her accomplishment on our behalf.

Postscript

In the summer of 1992, Robert Irig shaped for the Stratford Gallery and subsequent tour the wonderfully comprehensive exhibition showing the Moiseiwitsch contribution to the Stratford Festival. For the first time, Tanya overcame her immense reserve to be seen and heard in a video presentation. Recapturing such wonders as the actors' fortitude in wearing the great heavy robes and masks she designed for *Oedipus Rex*, she explained the reason why the central pillar of the Festival's main stage brings it to mystic union. It is the central point of the building that architect Robert Fairfield created around her original design.

This revelation underscored the vandalism that the 40th anniversary season committed on the stage, which had known destructive attempts before. For David William's production of *The Tempest*, Susan Benson (certainly one of the most talented and sensitive artists to succeed Moiseiwitsch) was tempted to saw off the front of the balcony, including that central pillar. She had also supplied some curious Easter Island sculptures in styrofoam to be used for scenic variation, which this stage never needs. One shudders to think that some kind of curse might fall upon her for desecrating a world theatre shrine, but she explains she had her fingers crossed. And in reverence of Tanya, the missing pillar is stored away in waiting.

As a designer of productions—as opposed to a designer of stages—Tanya Moiseiwitsch must suffer the theatre's curse of transience. Productions are discarded after their closing nights, even in festival theatres such as Stratford's and Niagara-on-the-Lake's. Only for opera are productions stored and brought out again or lent to other companies.

But to the Moiseiwitsch setting of Congreve's *The Double Dealer* for the National Theatre of Britain in 1978, a supreme contradiction of this self-destructive rule was issued. After the production left the repertory, she was informed that it would be kept in storage, awaiting the next revival of that play.

Her design for the Congreve costumes and setting well deserved that unique honour. Filling the difficult Olivier stage comfortably, the production's permanent setting was a miracle of entrances and exits, all demanded by the playwright. The design supplied an amazing variety of new entrances for its actors, always to advantage.

And the National supplied a dazzling cast of players to use them—including Dorothy Tutin, Michael Bryant, Nicky Henson, Sara Kestelman and Sir Ralph Richardson as Lord Touchwood, under Peter Wood's exuberant direction. A production well worth the storage, and the high respect implied.

Gordon Craig in Moscow, 1909
(autographed to H.W.W.)

Tanya Moiseiwitsch and Chinese lion dog,1980
photo by the author

Robert Edmond Jones's design for the street scene in *Faust*, 1928

Interior of Royal Alexandra Theatre, Toronto, 1973
photo courtesy Mirvish Productions

"Honest Ed" Mirvish, 1963

Ernest Rawley, c. 1965

Ernest Rawley

Born in Montreal in 1906. Joined Trans-Canada Theatres in 1921. Became press agent for Royal Alexandra Theatre in Toronto in 1924, and subsequently became theatre manager. Booked and promoted Canadian Opera Company, National Ballet of Canada, *My Fur Lady*, *Ti-Coq*, Théâtre du Nouveau Monde, Dominion Drama Festival finals, as well as the New Play Society, Jupiter Theatre, and *Spring Thaw*. International attractions included John Gielgud, Katharine Cornell, Alfred Lunt and Lynn Fontanne, Sadler's Wells Ballet. Transferred to New York Independent Booking Office in 1963. Died in Toronto in 1969.

EDWIN MIRVISH

Born in Virginia Beach, Virginia, in 1914. Educated in Toronto at King Edward School and Central Technical High School. Married Anne Kornhauser. Opened Honest Ed's discount department store. First theatre experience was watching Al Jolson appearing at the Royal Alexandra. Bought Royal Alexandra Theatre in 1963. Opened Ed's Warehouse, Old Ed's and Ed's Seafood restaurants. Bought London's Old Vic Theatre in 1983. Honours: CBE and Order of Canada. Awards from *Toronto Telegram*, Toronto Drama Bench and City of Toronto. With son David, built Princess of Wales Theatre in 1993.

Royal Alexandra's Men

This story is brief, but it captures a moment of world change through theatre. Its hero is not an actor, director, designer or critic, but a theatre manager. Ernest Rawley, an Irish Montrealer, was the proud manager of the Royal Alexandra Theatre in Toronto. He was largely responsible for its prominence in the circuit of Broadway road shows, the principal source of North American theatre in the post-war days. The Royal Alex was booked most of the year with attractions, including ballet, en route to New York or touring out from there. Later, Rawley's expertise was recognized by New York insiders when he became director of the Independent Booking Office, a New York agency on Times Square.

Largely because of his efforts, Toronto was an excellent theatre town, with prosperous, well-educated and moderately broad-minded audiences. The latter hesitation comes because the city's hotels, in deference to their American visitors, did not welcome black guests. Even the great soprano, Marian Anderson, who was registered at the Royal York Hotel, was asked to use the back entrance when visiting town to sing at Massey Hall.

Knowing this reluctance by local hotels, the advance agent for Gershwin's opera, *Porgy and Bess*, arranged for the cast to be billeted with members of the black congregations in town. Then the blizzard struck.

On the Sunday night that the *Porgy and Bess* company arrived by train, a great snow storm came across the lake.

Ernie Rawley, meeting the company at Union Station, led the black singers, dancers and actors through the tunnel under Front Street into the Royal York's lobby. At the registration desk, he demanded refuge for them all. Conjuring up some deep-rooted tradition of innkeepers, staff extended hospitality—although it was less because of tradition than because of Ernie Rawley's Irish belligerence.

So it was that this spunky theatre manager forced a stronghold of conservatism to break its own rules and join the struggle for civil rights. Perhaps as our reward, some members of that large collection of black talent remembered Canada's reputation for hospitality in the days of The Underground Railway, dating back to the American Civil War. The world was moved by the subsequent racial struggle, and a Toronto theatre had made a dramatic contribution on our behalf.

The Royal Alexandra Theatre, built by the young millionaire Cawthra Mulock in 1907, has bridged many changes towards greater independence in this country's self-expression through the most public of the arts. It survived the old stock theatre, which at one time gave Torontonians a generous choice of weekly shows, and also the vaudeville houses. The Royal Alex, as it became popularly known, maintained a steady flow of outside attractions to feed and develop the theatre-going habit.

The Royal Alex also launched into professionalism two of our major arts institutions—the Canadian Opera Company and the National Ballet of Canada—both intended as national companies, as their choice of names indicates. The theatre had been cautious in playing host to Canadian entertainment, but has to its credit *The Dumbells* and *The Army Show*, *Meet the Navy,* the

Dominion Drama Festival, the New Play Society and Jupiter Theatre; there were other individual creations too, including Gratien Gélinas's *Ti-Coq* (staged in 1949) and Tomson Highway's *Dry Lips Oughta Move to Kapuskasing* (staged in 1991).And when public interest turned from bread to circuses, such important musicals as *Hair* and *Les Miserables* settled there.

This rare continuity as a showcase, unmatched in all of Canada, I suggest, depended on its luck in management. Lawrence Soloman, who ruled from 1907 to 1937, trained the fighting Irishman, Ernie Rawley, who served the theatre from 1938 to 1963. He was followed by that most popular of storekeepers, "Honest Ed" Mirvish, joined later by his son, David.

That last transition was not without its humourous aspects, which I recite with great affection. Invited to give the citation when the Royal Alex was at long last recognized officially as a heritage treasure, I told the tale as it had been relayed to me by Rawley's second-in-command, Eddie Du Rocher. When the Cawthra estate decided to unload this property, Rawley decided he could not work under a new owner, whoever it might be. His expertise in booking shows had been established even beyond our boundaries. He was offered, and accepted, control of the Independent Booking Office in New York. While various consortiums were putting together their plans to take over the King Street edifice, Rawley grew impatient. He issued a press release, warning them that the Royal Alex was in danger of being demolished. This was accepted as very possible, since Her Majesty's Theatre in Montreal had gone that route, a parking lot replacing it.

When the first individual with ready cash declared himself, his offer was snapped up quickly. So Ed Mirvish won the hearts of all loyal Torontonians, rich and poor, as the saviour of this flagship theatre. Like a knight in shining armour, I proclaimed, Edwin Mirvish has enhanced his reputation and been rewarded internationally, for his purchase here encouraged him to acquire London's even more famous Old Vic.

I don't know what Ed Mirvish's reaction was when I told this story, for he was behind me on the platform built outside his theatre. But he need not have been upset, since, a few minutes later, a curtain was drawn on the plaque which now adorns the outer lobby of the Royal Alex. It set down, in letters of bronze, Ed Mirvish's part in saving the Royal Alexandra from demolition. The year was 1963, the price $215,000. Mirvish was lavish in its restoration. The refurbishing of architect John M. Lyle's beautiful interior was done by the leading Canadian interior decorator, Herbert Irvine, of Eaton's. Mirvish was to show the same care and even greater generosity (spending about two million pounds) in restoring the Old Vic in London, winning the gratitude of, among others, the Queen Mother. He was honoured appropriately in the next Honours List as Commander of the British Empire.

This chronicle of mounting success continued as the century wound down. When the age of big spectacles descended upon us, a worthy Mirvish rival appeared in the person of Garth Drabinsky, who refurbished the reclaimed movie palace, The Pantages, for his extravagantly promoted production of *The Phantom of the Opera.* And in north Toronto, North York launched another big auditorium, announcing its premiere production, *Show Boat*, for 1993.

What would be the effect, I wondered, on the Royal Alexandra's audiences, drawn from a wide-flung population, when one show occupied the theatre for as long as *Les Miserables* did? The Mirvishes, father and son, came up with a daring answer, breathtaking in the dim light of the nineties' recession: they built another theatre on King Street. The Princess of Wales Theatre, larger than the Royal Alex but in the same traditional conformation, will hold the long-running spectacles as long as they are popular, freeing the Royal Alex for its seasons of attractions on subscription—a system Ed Mirvish staunchly supports.

This arrangement was launched in May 1993 when another hit musical, *Miss Saigon*, was premiered. The Mirvish family's theatrical management seems guaranteed to continue triumphantly serving its large theatre public into the 21st century.

Some Notable Players

We nodded sagely in 1951 when we heard Charles Laughton as Galileo misquote the riposte, "Unhappy the land that has no hero." Of course, that line should be "Unhappy the land that needs a hero." Had Laughton used the word "star" for "hero," we might have stood our Canadian ground in protest. More sparsely populated a land back then, we felt the need for our own stars. Pity the land that lacks stars in its sky.

Canada's position on stardom has always resembled that of the United States on monarchy. All monarchs will be cheered, as long as they belong to somebody else. We were delighted to receive visiting stars, and did—from Kean to Bernhardt to Irving to Coquelin to Cornell to the Lunts to Barrault to Gielgud to Burton. But at home, we are suspicious of the breed.

The CBC reflected that national suspicion. Only one major dramatic talent achieved the exalted rank during its Golden Age of radio, and that was John Drainie. (Lorne Green was different. A CBC announcer, he didn't achieve stardom as an actor until he went to "the States.") Monarchs by nature must be seen in person, as the British know. Drainie, after his role as Galileo at the Jupiter Theatre, made few stage appearances. Once, when I'd drawn him to Stratford's attention, he called me in a rage about the minor roles it had offered to him. He flatly rejected them—and it.

At a time when the Stratford Festival was importing its first stars in Alec Guinness and Irene Worth—with James Mason, Paul Scofield, Siobhan McKenna, Alan Bates, Maggie Smith and Brian Bedford still in its future—we began to notice that Quebec was finding its own stars. It had for some time, encouraged by the isolation of language. But it remained for Gratien Gélinas to shine brightly enough to catch our eye.

The legend of Gratien Gélinas is worth repeating again. It brought awe when recited at the Arts and Letters Club the last time he acted in Toronto and was honoured with a luncheon. The play was his own, *The Passion of Narcisse Mondoux.*

Born in Saint-Tite, Quebec, he took his classical studies at the Collège de Montréal, organizing La Troupe des Anciens afterwards. At that time, he also made his debut in English, playing Dr. Caius for the Montreal Repertory Theatre. Radio turned him professional, and for radio he created his character of the shrewd little gamin, Fridolin. The subsequent success of the Fridolin revues encouraged him to develop one sketch full length, which became *Ti-Coq.* A huge Montreal success, this sad history of an illegitimate young soldier (which gave the lie to Olivier's Quebecois caricature on film) scored with English-speaking audiences in translation in Montreal, before touring to Toronto, Chicago and New York. Toronto cheered its study of Quebec isolation at the Royal Alexandra Theatre. New York—both critics and audience—rejected it. But Toronto, to its credit, welcomed him back again, defying Broadway's edict.

Montreal honoured Gélinas with his own theatre, La Comédie-Canadienne, where he starred in his own plays, *Bousille et les justes* and *Yesterday the Children Were Dancing*, which touched on contemporary separatism. (The latter play was cheered louder in Charlottetown than in Montreal.) Stratford made him King of France in Michael Langham's 1956 production of *Henry V*—uniting its best players with the best of Montreal in its strongest cast ever. Ottawa officially honoured this little comedian with his enormous gift for pathos by making him chairman of the Canadian Film Development Corporation in 1969, as well as giving him the Order of Canada to match his other honourary degrees. I had honoured him first, as *Gazette* critic, by introducing him to my English-speaking readers when he did his *Fridolinades* at the Monument National. Of course, he richly repaid their interest, both in understanding and in unique performance—a distinct stardom discovered.

So, while Stratford was still building an acting company, Quebec was searching out stars. Le Théâtre du Nouveau Monde, which played in the Orpheum Theatre before it inherited La Comédie-Canadienne, produced two undisputed actor/managers in Jean Gascon and Jean-Louis Roux, as well as celebrities such as Guy Hoffmann and Olivette Thibault. L'Equipe had, in Pierre Dagenais, an undeniable star as actor/manager, while from its ranks came two actress/managers in Yvette Brind'Amour of Théâtre du Rideau Vert fame and the beloved Denise Pelletier, for whom a theatre was named after her untimely death in 1976.

Taking heart from Stratford's popular success, theatres

were springing up as ornaments to civilized cities. We called them "regional" in some pseudo-metropolitan fashion. In Toronto, which never accepted the term, two actors/managers, Murray and Donald Davis, followed Dora and Mavor Moore's New Play Society and the Jupiter Theatre. They offered continuous seasons, the like of which had not been enjoyed locally since the stock theatres had prevailed early in the century. (Mavor Moore reminds me that local talents such as Jane Mallett had to go to auditions in New York to be engaged to play in their own city.)

The Davises, graduates of Robert Gill's memorable regime at the University of Toronto's Hart House Theatre, first ran their summer operation, The Straw Hat Players, before launching the Crest Theatre's three week long productions in 1954. They and their sister, the striking Barbara Chilcott, played leading roles in a varied repertory, one which included new Canadian plays as well as imports, largely by British playwrights. Robertson Davies wrote *A Jig for the Gypsy* for their first season, and J.B. Priestley *The Glass Cage*, which this handsome trio took to London's West End after its opening in Toronto. The Crest companies were strong, drawing on Gill graduates such as Charmion King and the darling of the Straw Hats, Kate Reid. Gill basically trained professional actors, other Gill graduates being William Hutt, Eric House, Anna Cameron, Ted Follows, David Gardner and Hal Jackman. (Tall and lean, Jackman once told me that he gave up theatre because he believed his height was against him. He went into business and emerged as Lieutenant Governor of Ontario, where height is an advantage.)

I have happy personal memories of several actors, in part because I directed them for the Crest: of Donald Davis in *Come Back, Little Sheba*, with Amelia Hall and Deborah Peddie; of Murray Davis in *The Prisoner*, with Douglas Campbell; and of Barbara Chilcott in *A Jig for the Gypsy*, with Max Helpmann and Eric House. Yet I retain the impression that the brothers made their name as managers/actors rather than actors/managers, an old-fashioned distinction. Both Donald and Barbara went on after the Crest collapsed (no credit to the arts councils there); Donald won international notice in Beckett's *Krapp's Last Tape* while Barbara scored as Katharine in *The Taming of the Shrew* at Stratford and on through to Hagar in *The Stone Angel*. But the Crest came nearer to stars with several others: Betty Leighton, who had appeared earlier at the Canadian Repertory Theatre; Austin Willis and "That Hamilton Woman," Barbara, in revue there. Nor should we ever forget Martha Buhs, straight out of the National Theatre School, who later became better known as Martha Henry; or Marilyn Lightstone, the Crest's last star as Hedda Gabler.

In Ottawa, Amelia Hall was recognized as manager/actress rather than the more starry position, despite her successes in *The Glass Menagerie*, *Emily Carr* and *Victoria Regina*. She went on, however, to the Crest and Stratford, being Alec Guinness's Lady Anne, and thus the first actress to step onto the Stratford stage. Her career was long and rewarding, with many of us sharing Stratford's great affection for "Millie" Hall. Her career ended after she had played Madame Pernelle in *Tartuffe* on that stage and on television, then scored the best performance in the Festival's *Separate Tables* at the Royal Alexandra Theatre in Toronto. In December 1984, after sending off her Christmas cards, she died peacefully in her sleep, leaving detailed instructions for the proper funeral of a leading Canadian actress. As good as was her entrance onto Stratford's stage, trailing black velvet, Amelia Hall's exit was equally superb, and she was deeply mourned.

Ontario's other festival of classical mandate (though more light-hearted), the Shaw Festival at Niagara-on-the-Lake, has also been a director's theatre, but with fewer imported stars—though one remembers Ian Richardson's John Tanner and Jessica Tandy's Lady Utterword in this category. After Paxton Whitehead's inspired playing of farce, applied even to Shaw, the Festival has seen outstanding talents such as Tony Van Bridge, an actor/manager too, there; Douglas Rain and William Hutt, stars borrowed from Stratford; and Frances Hyland and Nicola Cavendish in architect Ron Thom's fine House of Shaw. But if there have been major star contributions, one would think more immediately of its actor/manager Christopher Newton or perhaps of its prize designer, Cameron Porteous. Both of Ontario's festivals have been accounted "designer's theatres" by outsiders. Canada sometimes seems perverse in refusing the star actor top place on its stage, even when dealing in masterworks patently composed for starry interpreters.

If the regional theatres preferred to put their hopes in directors—sometimes star directors like Manitoba Theatre Centre's John Hirsch, but more often merely reliable commodities—the "alternate theatres," which ringed around the bigger establishments like moons, were also dedicated to directorial emphasis, though there have been many notable pioneer performers. On occasion, we find phenomena such as Jane Mallett at Theatre Passe Muraille, R.H. Thomson invading the company stronghold of George Luscombe's Toronto Workshop Productions, or Brent Carver at the Poor Alex. But for the most part, the alternates all across the country followed the ruling bent of the regionals: no stars.

An exception, Tarragon Theatre's Bill Glassco, did after a while swing away from the nurturing of playwrights to favour the players. Notable among Tarragon's star turns were Clare Coulter, daughter of the playwright, the unique Jackie Burroughs and Richard Monette, whose performance of Michael Tremblay's *Hosanna* was a most remarkable star turn. But Monette found his path elevated when he turned director and went on to the highest position Canada offers in that category as artistic director of the Stratford Festival.

One is reminded that Monette's fellow Montrealer, the brilliant Jean Gascon, flourished as director rather than actor, despite the histrionic impact he made in Strindberg's *Dance of Death* or Molière's *Don Juan.* If there is a statue raised to him (or two, as I suggested at a McGill convocation), it will be as the artist who headed the country's two major theatres of their day—Le Théâtre du Nouveau Monde (1951) and the Stratford Festival (1968)—with a nod to his leadership roles at the National Arts Centre in Ottawa and Edmonton's Citadel Theatre. These were the "star turns" which crowned this brilliant actor's career.

Gascon's death in 1988 at age 67 came after he had completed a guest production for Stratford of the musical, *My Fair Lady*—a remarkable job of fitting something onto the wrong kind of stage for it. His musicality, always present in the Gascon career, flourished at the end. Yet neither music nor theatre was his first choice of a career, which was medicine.

On his death, Eric McLean quoted from a *Gazette* interview which I had done with Gascon much earlier: "Each time in my life . . . there was a great change, something happened. A miracle. When I decided to take time off interning, to see if theatre was my life, I got a scholarship, a French government scholarship."

The French cultural attaché in Canada had seen Jean Gascon as an actor with Les Compagnons de Saint-Laurent, the student company of Père Emile Legault. Already he'd played the aging Theseus opposite the Phaedre of the celebrated Parisian actress, Ludmilla Pitoeff. (I had travelled around Mount Royal to see this astonishing production at the Université de Montréal. Here was an actor!)

Back from Paris in 1951, Gascon founded Le Théâtre du Nouveau Monde, our premier Quebecois theatre, involving other notables such as Jean-Louis Roux, Jean Duceppe, Yvette Brind'Amour, Marcel Dubé, Roger Lemelin and Guy Hoffmann. His success with it won him the Molson Award in 1966. Two years later, he returned to head the Stratford Festival, our premier English theatre.

At his death, both founding cultures mourned his loss equally. Choked with emotion, Gratien Gélinas called the loss "irreparable," while his Stratford successor of the day, John Neville, declared his legacy "incalculable." His country had recognized his contributions at Stratford and the National Arts Centre with the Royal Bank Award and the Prix du Quebec; his 1967 Order of Canada was elevated to Companion in 1975. Jean Gascon was one Canadian star whose worth did not go unnoticed.

But we observe that the natural growth of theatre from coast to coast instinctively followed a no-star policy, which is obviously more democratic—but when was the theatre ever democratic? In Canada, it is an aristocratic institution, with the aristocrats off stage still. Let me risk a metaphor: having previously observed Canadians up close, Tyrone Guthrie arrived to stage *Oedipus Rex* in 1954 with a design plan that demanded both masks and the high cothurni for his principals' footwear. Yet, when he had staged the work previously in Tel Aviv and Helsinki, his actors seemed to need neither.

Guthrie instinctively sized us up when he first arrived to establish a classical theatre in Stratford. With the help of Tanya Moiseiwitsch, he created a director's theatre. (Laurence Olivier, visiting briefly, spotted that there was no place in it for a star actor.) Guthrie's first year's *All's Well That Ends Well* was more successful than his *Richard III,* with Alec Guinness as the blood-thirsty Plantagenet, maybe because of that choice. *All's Well* paved the way for the distinguished record of the Canadian Stratford in Shakespeare's company plays—unmatched anywhere or, I venture to claim, at any time.

If our measure as a "company" rather than a star struck land has been taken by experts like Guthrie, why are we so attracted by the stars of other lands? Have we recognized the great value of the star figures to any theatre,

Frank Peddie with the Davis family, Barbara (Chilcott), Murray and Donald, 1957
photo Robert C. Ragsdale, F.R.P.S.

Amelia Hall at Stratford, 1956

Gratien Gélinas in *Ti-Coq*, 1949

R.H. Thomson in *The Real Thing*, by Tom Stoppard, 1985

but been too hesitant to compete? That premise may be exasperating but it is not too fantastic. Eventually, if theatre is to serve its original purpose—to give its audiences the speakers who voice their highest as well as darkest concerns—we know we must have our own major voices to speak to us and for us. There is surely no need to avoid that fact any longer.

We don't regret those luminaries from abroad who have shown us what stardom means; but we do resent losing all those bright talents of our own to foreign stages and screens. Had we been able to keep them at home, what a starry heaven we would be observing today! At this point, a practical voice will undoubtedly cut in with: "And how much less well-off they would be today!" Certainly I must answer, "Ay, there's the rub." Do we need our stars enough to pay for them? Can we afford our greatest talents? We ask such sacrifices of the ones who stay that we are bound to feel grateful when a producer or director scoops up one for exploitation abroad at a proper salary. (As I write, a splendid example is given by the gifted Brent Carver in *Kiss of the Spider Woman.*)

And then there is that other challenge, which I faced as a newsman. Why don't we publicize our star players when we find them, as we do in hockey and baseball? A nation that postpones broadcasts of the national news when teams get close to the final competitions is frivolous enough to relish news of the best stage players too.

We have no answers, save that we are a young country. We look hopefully to the huge audiences drummed up expensively for franchised spectacles in our largest auditioria. Yet some of us declare that our aspirations for theatre lie elsewhere. As Shaw wrote, "the human spirit demands optimism." So we demand our own theatre's creativity be given full attention.

But stay! If you sniff the theatrical air keenly, you may get a whiff of the old stardust, catch the edge of the star's spotlight out of the corner of your eye, or hear the echo of the commanding voice. Having trained our directors and served them well with stage production and lighting, we are now ready to receive our stars at the centre of our stages. I welcome them.

R.H. THOMSON

Born in Toronto in 1947. Educated at University of Toronto, National Theatre School, London Academy of Music and Drama. Debut at Rideau Hall (age four). Professional debut at Centaur Theatre in Montreal. Married in 1984, two sons. Plays include *Hamlet*, *The Jail Diary of Albie Sachs*, *The Comedians*, *Waiting for Godot, The Real Thing, Death and the Maiden.* Films and television include *Glory Enough for All*, *Charlie Grant's War*, *The Quarrel*, *Ticket to Heaven.*

Doubting Thomson

Robert Thomson—R. H. to accommodate Equity membership lists—represents the new breed of Canadian actor, the long-awaited Canadian who sets his sights on the Canadian audience. Equally representative would be Monique Mercure, Gordon Pinsent, Eric Peterson, Jean-Louis Roux, Nicola Cavendish, Rod Beattie, Jackie Burroughs, Norman Browning and an increasing number of others. But R. H. Thomson is the one who fits into my master plan for these "theatricals." Fits, if only on a technicality.

The "doubting" of that title should be explained, if you don't know him or his refusal to take anything for granted. He has that from his father, University of Toronto Professor W. S. "Woody" Thomson, just as he has his vocation of theatre from his mother, Cicely. Both were redoubtable residents of Richmond Hill, Ontario, for many years.

One summer, I emerged from a London theatre uplifted because I had seen a new production of Shaw's *Pygmalion*, which had Diana Rigg as an aggressive Eliza and Alec McCowen as a speech expert whose ideal woman was his mother. I was elated that Shaw's comedy had survived its musical version (*My Fair Lady*) and, in accommodating women's liberation, was proving the adaptability that assures its place as a classic. As I came out of the theatre, I encountered a familiar tall and lanky redheaded young Canadian.

"Robert! You here? How are you enjoying London theatre?" To which he answered gloomily, "Not much." It was the same kind of reluctance to be impressed that characterized his later foray into Canada's sacred Stratford Festival.

He recently explained to me that, after going to the University of Toronto (he was "too young" for General Arts but won honours when he switched to Science), he had settled for the National Theatre School to get on with his career. He actually liked some of it (Powys Thomas's courses) but left Montreal after two years for the London Academy of Music and Dramatic Arts. He says it was a chip on his shoulder against American acting which took him to London. Once there, he fell in with the American students at LAMDA and began to despise the "pro-wy" English acting.

He joined Shakespeare and Co., a group headed for America after rehearsing with John Barton at Stratford-upon-Avon. An American tour of *The Taming of the Shrew* followed; when it was over, he joined the New York Shakespeare Festival briefly. Unexpectedly, Sam Cohen, a New York agent, told him what he wanted to hear: if he wanted to learn to act Shakespeare, he'd better go home to Canada. He had already, it may be said, been impressed on a visit home by Carol Bolt's *Red Emma*, as staged by Toronto Free Theatre. He particularly liked Toronto Free's sense of communal theatre. Home he came, starting out in Winnipeg to build his career.

Sometime about then he made another of the excursions seemingly obligatory for Canadian actors of the day: he went to Los Angeles. But once there, he found the offers coming from home far more interesting than what was offered in California. His agent there complained that, whenever he needed to set up an audition for his client, R.H. was back in Toronto. He was, in fact, already charting out the kind of career he wanted for himself.

George Luscombe's well-researched documentation of the Canadian involvement in the Spanish Civil War, *The Mac-Paps,* was a case in point. Robert had a political affinity for that as he had for playing Albie Sachs, the South African activist, also at Luscombe's Toronto Workshop Productions. His own left-of-centre polities were a major influence on his career. He also enjoyed giving a wicked impersonation of Canadian Prime Minister Joe Clark, in a play called *Hand to Hand*, an unusual exercise for him.

Plaudits for these and other appearances won him an invitation to Ontario's Stratford. But he did not fit into a company which still favoured the traditional British style of acting Shakespeare, either as a very sincere Mark Antony in *Julius Caesar* or as a comical Simple in *The Merry Wives of Windsor*. He felt much more at home playing Hamlet at Toronto Free Theatre for Guy Sprung, which swung in quite another direction. Yet his doubts about traditional histrionic form have not shut him off from exploring the more formal styles of French classical theatre, for in 1992 he played Racine for Opera Atelier.

Meanwhile, without great need of Los Angeles, R.H. was building a public for himself in Canadian film and television; he graduated to roles such as Banting in *Glory Enough For All* and played opposite Saul Rubinek in *Ticket to Heaven* and *The Quarrel*. (To play the renegade Jew in the latter, he was referred to the Montreal poet, Irving Layton, for guidance, and proved a good match for Rubinek.) In portraying a discoverer of insulin, a saviour of Nazi victims, or a Prince Edward Islander in *The Road to Avonlea*, he was being recognized as a most suitable Canadian star—somebody plainly serious, even dogged, uncompromising, modest, helpful to others and incorruptible.

That's why Canadians like him: he is so much like themselves as they see themselves. "Quintessentially Canadian," *The Globe and Mail* labelled him in Liam Lacey's profile of June 6, 1992. His colleagues agreed, voting him winner of Gemini, Genie and Dora Mavor Moore Awards. Another *Globe* writer, Rick Salutin, confers the *coup d'honneur*, stating that Thomson's performances "have the ring of truth that transcends acting." To which Thomson replies: "An old acting teacher of mine said it this way: the text is male, the actor female, the character is their child. At the end of every play, that child dies. A life has been shown from beginning to end. That's why actors have been traditionally marginalized, kept out of the church and so on. Because they're creating something, and only God is supposed to do that."

But Robert was not about to decline into a television star. His work for the stage has precedence in his calendar. He has covered that territory well, starting with Eddie Gilbert's Manitoba Theatre Centre in *Black Comedy,* Malcolm Black directing; affiliating himself with Toronto Free Theatre for Ondaatje's *The Collected Works of Billy the Kid*, directed by Martin Kinch, scaling the heights of Ed Mirvish's Royal Alexandra Theatre to star in Tom Stoppard's *The Real Thing*, which Guy Sprung directed.

Through all this, he has built a true Canadian identity, and is very much part of that sense of communal theatre. He stood alongside Karen Kain and other such notables of the artistic community to remind Ottawa of the place the arts must have in shaping a new constitution. He even undertook the artistic direction of the du Maurier World Theatre Festival to convert that semi-annual event to his convictions about world solidarity.

I had been studying the rise of this true Canadian star for a while, having had several vantage points along the way. Not only could I review his work for *The Globe and Mail*, I also had an opportunity to direct him in his growing years. Through the University Alumnae Drama Club—to which his mother, Cicely, was a major contributor—we explored a new play by Jack Cunningham called *Aperitif*, in which he played the leading role. At Hart House, when the ancients of Athens came trundling down the aisle for the new Centre for the Study of Drama at the University of Toronto, young Bob Thomson led them in Aristophanes' *Lysistrata.*

Years later, he invited me to lunch and to serve on his advisory board for the du Maurier World Theatre Festival of 1992. That gave me an opportunity to see how he had grown in confidence, still taking nothing for granted but now taking responsibility for artistic policy. He spent much of 1991 in a solo exploration of Japan and the European theatre festivals to select the companies which, exotic though they were, expressed his demand for solidarity. His introduction to the 1992 program speaks directly for him: "The voices which you will hear in these eighteen works are infectious, charged with the vitality of peoples in ascendancy. The voices are challenging, original, comedic, exhilarating, wry and hysterical. But above all, they are energized by their deep commitment to the journey of the human spirit."

There follows a list of attractions from Romania, Brazil, Lithuania, Japan, France and Britain—but also, equally balanced, from Canada itself, proving the point that this country has won its place in world theatre at last.

As I have been trying to prove, world theatre was always in touch with Canada, even though Canadians never thought it was. So it is that R.H. Thomson has found his place in this collection of world theatricals. I can think of no better representative of the new Canadian Theatre to include among the others, past and present, who are my concern here. And I thank him warmly for taking time out of his busy Canadian career to write a foreword for an old friend and colleague.

BIBLIOGRAPHY

Benson, Eugene and Conolly, L. W., eds. *The Oxford Companion to Canadian Theatre.* Toronto, Oxford, New York: Oxford University Press, 1989.

Bernhardt, Sarah. *Memories of My Life.* New York: D. Appleton & Company, 1907.

Billy Rose Theatre Collection in the New York Public Library for the Performing Arts (at Lincoln Centre).

Blum, Daniel. *Pictorial History of the American Theatre.* New York: Greenberg Publishers, 1950.

Boland, Maureen. *Wilde's Devoted Friend.* Oxford: Lennard Publishing, 1990.

Collard, Edgar Andrew. *The Gazette,* Montreal.

Craig, Edward. *Gordon Craig: The Story of His Life.* London: Victor Gollancz Ltd., 1968.

Davies, Robertson. *Murther and Walking Spirits.* Toronto: McClelland and Stewart, 1991.

Ellmann, Richard. *Oscar Wilde.* London: Hamish Hamilton, Ltd., 1987.

Eyman, Scott. *Mary Pickford.* Toronto: HarperCollins, 1990.

Forsyth, James. *Tyrone Guthrie: A Biography.* London: Hamish Hamilton, 1976.

Garebian, Keith. *William Hutt: A Theatre Portrait.* Oakville: Mosaic Press, 1988.

Graham, Franklin. *Histrionic Montreal.* Montreal: John Lovell & Son, Publishers, 1892.

Hayman, Ronald. *John Gielgud.* New York: Random House, 1971.

Holroyd, Michael. *Bernard Shaw. Vol. II: The Pursuit of Power; Vol. III: The Line of Fantasy.* London: Chatto & Windus, 1989, 1991.

Jefferson, Joseph. *The Autobiography of Joseph Jefferson.* New York: The Century Company, 1890.

Jones, Donald. "Historical Toronto," *The Toronto Star,* May 21, 1988.

Jones, Robert Edmond. *Drawings for the Theatre.* New York: Theatre Arts, Inc., 1925.

Komisarjevsky, Theodore. *Myself and the Theatre.* New York: F. P. Dutton & Co., Inc., 1930.

Lee, Betty. *Love and Whisky: The Story of The Dominion Drama Festival.* Toronto: Simon & Pierre, 1982.

Le Vay, John. *Margaret Anglin, A Stage Life.* Toronto: Simon & Pierre, 1989.

Lillie, Beatrice. *Every Other Inch A Lady.* Garden City, New York: Doubleday & Company, Inc., 1972.

Martin-Harvey, Sir John. *Autobiography of Sir John Martin-Harvey*. London: Sampson Low, Marston & Co., Ltd., n.d.

Molloy, J. Fitzgerald. *Life and Adventures of Edmund Kean, Tragedian*. Covent Garden, London: Downey & Co., Limited, 1897.

Morris, Clara. *Life on the Stage*. London: Isbister & Co. Ltd., 1902.

"New Hamlet and 'Hamlet'." (unsigned) *The Globe*, September 26, 1936.

Patterson, Tom and Gould, Allan. *First Stage: The Making of the Stratford Festival.* Toronto: McClelland and Stewart, 1987.

Peters, Margo. *Mrs. Pat: The Life of Mrs. Patrick Campbell.* London, Sydney, Toronto: The Bodley Head, 1984.

Pickford, Mary. *Sunshine and Shadow*. Garden City, New York: Doubleday & Company, Inc., 1955.

Primm, John. *Komisarjevsky's Life and Work*. An unpublished manuscript.

Ross, Robert Baldwin. Preface to *The Importance of Being Earnest* (A Souvenir Edition). London, 1910.

Sayler, Oliver M. *The Russian Theatre*. New York: Little, Brown and Company, 1920.

Sherrin, Ned. *Ned Sherrin's Theatrical Anecdotes*. London: Virgin Books, 1992.

Volker, Klaus. *Brecht: A Biography*. London and Boston: Marion Boyars, 1979.

Wagner, Anton, ed. *Contemporary Canadian Theatre*. Toronto: Simon & Pierre, 1985.

Walker, Hugh. *The O'Keefe Centre*. Toronto: Key Porter Books, 1991.

Whittaker, Herbert. "America's Leading Lady" in *The Globe Magazine*. Toronto: *The Globe and Mail*, September 7, 1957.

Whittaker, Herbert. *The Stratford Festival 1953-1957*. Toronto: Clarke, Irwin & Company Limited, 1958.

Wilson, Francis. *John Wilkes Booth*. Boston and New York: Houghton Mifflin Company, 1929.

Windeler, Robert. *Sweetheart: The Story of Mary Pickford*. New York, Washington: Praeger Publishers, 1974.

BIOGRAPHICAL NOTE

Born in Montreal in 1910, Herbert Whittaker attended L'Ecole des Beaux Arts, and became a stage designer while studying there. He soon went on to designing and directing plays for several amateur and semi-professional groups in the city—including Everyman Players, the YM/YWHA, Montreal Repertory Theatre and the Shakespeare Society of Montreal—before becoming the junior critic for theatre and film at *The Gazette.*

In 1949, he moved to Toronto to be drama, film and dance critic for *The Globe and Mail*, always championing developments in Canadian theatre. While chronicling events on the boards from his seat in the audience, he continued his career as director and designer, mounting productions for Hart House, Jupiter, The Crest and University Alumnae theatres, and the Canadian Players. He retired from the *Globe* in 1975.

Whittaker's contributions have been recognized with the Order of Canada, several honourary degrees, and the first honourary memberships in Actors' Equity Association and the Association of Canadian Designers. Whittaker continues his efforts on behalf of Canadian theatre from his downtown Toronto apartment, whose green walls display a portion of his remarkable collection of theatrical portraits and mementos.

> *Mr. Whittaker's influence on the Canadian stage is as diverse as it is profound. His own art and craft directly contributed to the professionalization of Canadian theatre before and after the war; his criticism, urging theatrical expression of the national spirit with international performance standards, challenged our artists, as one member of the theatrical family might another, to settle for nothing but the best; and his generous recognition and encouragement of talent, to say nothing of his tireless support of such organizations as the Dominion Drama Festival, the National Arts Centre, and the Toronto Drama Bench, leaves countless artists and theatergoers forever in his debt.*
>
> (Excerpt from an address by Professor John Ripley, on the occasion of McGill University conferring on honourary degree on Herbert Whittaker, November 1991)

INDEX

Boldface numbers refer to pictures
Boldface Italics refer to titles